UNIQUE FRIEND 2

AKASH MISHRA

"I would like to express my sincere gratitude to my amazing parents for their unwavering support and motivation in every situation life has presented me. I could not have achieved this without your constant encouragement and belief in me. Mom and Dad, your love and support mean everything to me. Thank you for everything."

Mom and Dad, I love you.

Contents

Contents

Contents

Acknowledgements

I would like to express my heartfelt gratitude to everyone who supported me in bringing this book to reality.

First and foremost, I would like to thank myself for not giving up despite many problems. I would like to thank my family and friends for their constant support and suggestions, and I am grateful to have you in my life.

I would like to thank my editor and proofreader, Afreen Nazeer, for your expert guidance. Your insight and suggestions helped shape this book into its best possible form. Your attention to details was invaluable and I am grateful for your contributions to the final product.

Also, I would like to thank Mannan Khan for creating my website and enabling me to connect with my audiance one on one.

To all of you, thank you for your invaluable contributions to this book. I am deeply grateful for your help and support, and I couldn't have done it without you.

Prologue

The storyline revolves around the moment when Anjali walked away from Aryan, leaving him heartbroken. Aryan's life has been shattered ever since Anjali walked out on him. He felt completely lost, like he had never felt before, as she had always been his source of motivation, support, and his only 'Unique Friend' who truly understood him. However, everything changed when he crossed paths with Divya.

Divya, the new CEO of Anjali's company, is a force of nature in his life, bringing both the power of a thunderstorm and the warmth of a ray of sunshine.

The story revolves around Divya, Aryan, and Jahnavi, with their interactions shaping the premises.

At first glance, Jahnavi appeared to be just another ordinary college student, but as the story progressed, her presence in Aryan's life became more prominent.

Get ready for a thrilling ride, because as the story progresses, it will spiral into a frenzy of insane and unpredictable twists and turns.

Through the pages of this book, we will witness how the mere presence or absence of one individual can have a profound impact on one's entire existence. How love, obsession, and jealousy shape the lives of each character of this story.

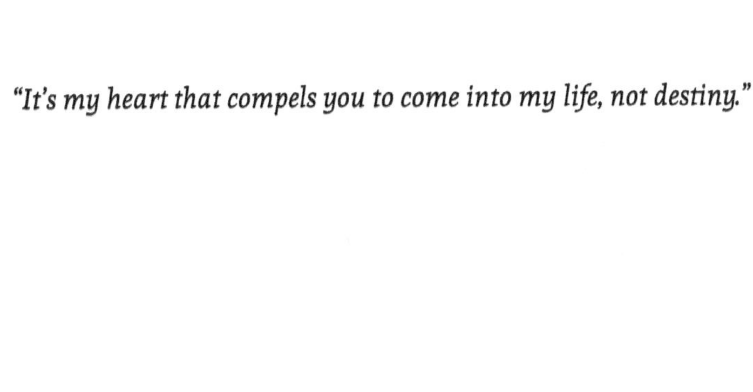

"It's my heart that compels you to come into my life, not destiny."

xiii

1

Chapter One

Mr. Brijesh Pandey and his partners wait for someone at an open rooftop restaurant. Mr. Rakesh Kumar Mishra, the owner of a small NGO, arrives and presents an impressive new project. It has the potential for a significant output with minimal input, especially if it receives government approval, which could multiply it by 10.

Mr. Pandey requested the blueprint, but he didn't bring it with him until he finally revealed his desire to have the assignment under his company's name.

He agreed, but with one condition: "This project aims to improve the health and status of the underprivileged. I have a good strategy and you have great resources; I get 30% of the profit for needy people, and you can have the rest."

"As a businessman, I prioritize my profit," Mr. Pandey interrupted. "I'll ensure your plan succeeds, but I need to profit from it first. Once I've recouped my investment, I can consider helping those in need. Don't worry, you'll get your fair share immediately."

Mr. Mishra responded, "I may not be as successful as you, but what I have is enough for me. I just want what I ask for, and you will surely earn more than you can imagine."

Aryan arrives on his modified bike under the hotel, holding the blueprint his father requested. Before delivering it, he examined the print and took out a pen. As his father approached, he quickly made the changes he had seen and took the hand of an unknown girl who was passing by. He hid behind her while placing the blueprint on her back to make the final correction. Once finished, he turned the unknown girl around and handed the print to his father.

Once his father departed, the unfamiliar girl released her hand from his grasp and proceeded to accompany Mr. Rakesh to the hotel. Aryan, sensing tension, followed her lead, but she disappeared suddenly in the crowd, leaving him behind.

As she enters the hotel, she waits for the elevator. Suddenly, a few strange men also arrive and stand behind her. When the elevator doors opened, there were more men inside, which made her suspicious, so she opted for the stairs. In a rush, she searched for an emergency exit and took cover behind the wall. After some time, she glanced outside and felt relieved to see the clear track. However, as soon as she took her first step, she collided with Aryan, who had been waiting for her and wanted to see her face while expressing gratitude for her support earlier.

Aryan greeted the lady and noticed an object aiming at her, so he shielded her by standing in front and saw a group of unfamiliar men signaling for the lady to be handed over. Aryan, feeling tense, asked the lady, "I didn't know you had such a big fan base, but I need your autograph before you can let go of my hand." Saying this, he quickly performed a series of tricks to rescue the girl from the mob and rushed upstairs.

While distracting most of the crew with a fight, he cleared a path for the lady to run away. She ran quickly and opened the door to escape but found more men coming towards her. Aryan emerged before her and shielded her by confronting the attackers, allowing them to flee towards another exit, but they were soon cornered by armed men, leaving no escape route.

Aryan tightly holds the girl's hand as he grips a pointed object in his other hand, engaging in a serious fight with the crew. Despite getting badly hurt, he refuses to let go of the girl's hand and does everything to protect her. Eventually, they reach the rooftop where there is a single door. Aryan covered the girl on his back to create an escape route.

As she opened the door, she discovered more armed men. Surprisingly, instead of attacking her, they attacked the other crew. Aryan, confused, turned around to find his father and a few businessmen waiting. With fear in her voice, the unknown girl ran towards Mr. Panday and held onto him tightly, saying, "I am scared."

Mr. Pandey gently touched her forehead and commanded his men to bring everyone down. While asking this, the entire building was held hostage and in front of everyone, he commanded the execution of those who attempted to harm his daughter, who clung to her father in fear. They then approached Aryan, but she intervened and saved him by saying, "He's the one who saved me."

Mr. Pandey was about to halt his men when he witnessed Aryan effortlessly taking down two of them, leaving him astonished. This was the first time Mr. Pandey had seen Aryan, an intermediate student, who displayed immense bravery in confronting any challenge. He was impressed and asked, "Son, what's your name? You've got guts."

"He's my son, Aryan Mishra," Mr. Mishra responded. "He arrived here with the blueprint and rescued your precious daughter."

Mr. Pandey glanced at Aryan and asked, "Do you have any wishes?"

Silently, Aryan took the blueprint from his father's hand and showed it to the crew. They were impressed by the modified details. Mr. Mishra becomes angry and tells him, "I've already made it clear that I don't want your opinion since it doesn't prioritize the welfare of the less fortunate."

Mr. Pandey interrupts Mr. Mishra and compliments his son's plan, suggesting that his son also has profit in mind. However, Mr. Mishra's concern is only for the welfare of the poor. Mr. Pandey then asks Aryan what he expects in return for the project. Aryan proposed, "In exchange for 80% of the profit, I'll give you 3 additional projects that will yield greater profits. So, what's your decision?"

Mr. Pandey responded, "You're much smarter than I expected, but I want this project and its profit. If you try to oppose me, I'll take it forcefully."

Aryan abruptly ripped the project, telling his father, "Even though you asked for only 50% of the share, he still opposed it. So, I tried with 80% and they are still opposing. I don't think they have enough money to buy our idea, so it's best if we leave and find another partner who can invest in our plan." and were leaving.

Mr. Pandey warned them, saying, "Your plan won't succeed because I'll take it away before you can even start."

Aryan stopped and replied, his voice filled with determination, "Uncle, there's no need for such worries. This project is already patented, so it's protected. But I promise you, I'll make it even more powerful, just like my father wanted."

Aryan approached Mr. Pandey before he left, glancing at his frightened daughter, who clung to her father. Aryan, since their first encounter, hasn't seen her face, but tried to reassure her by saying, "I believe you are safe now. Bye Miss Pandey"

As she saw him leave, Anjali held her father even tighter and decided to have Aryan in her life forever.

2
Chapter Two

Present time,

Divya closes the diary after reading about Aryan saving Anjali during their first meeting, pondering on their unknown connection. Despite this, the father refused to express gratitude towards him; instead, he prioritized that secret project over his own daughter and quietly wondered, "What makes that project so special?"

While contemplating this, she noticed the paper sticking halfway out of the diary. Seeing Aryan's sketch brought back memories of how he gazed at her with tear-filled eyes while listening to the remorseful news about his aunt, lost in thoughts of his past life with Anjali.

The following day, Divya walked to the manager's room and gazed at the chair where her deceased aunt once sat. Everyone greeted their new boss, but she seemed lost. As she sat down, she carefully examined the college records, specifically focusing on Aryan's records. She diligently searched every detail of his whereabouts and encounters with her elder sister, only to be shocked by the absence of any information. Anjali refuses to share Aryan with anyone, which makes Divya desperate about their love as everything has been erased and she seems anxious about it.

Divya departed to the palace and searched for clues in Anjali's room. She eventually found a drive. She begins collecting each individual detail about Aryan by examining them one by one. While watching the recording, she discovered a hidden folder containing recordings of their romance. Reluctantly, she decided to watch the recordings, desperate for Aryan's love. The recordings captured every moment and interaction they had in college. While watching the recording, her focus is mainly on Aryan - how he holds her and takes care of her - which excites her so much that she turns off the recording.

Afterwards, she picked up the diary and continued reading, discovering that Anjali had no boundaries in hurting him, yet he never opposed her. Instead, he loved and cared for her rough side even more than his mystery girl. Anjali's description of Aryan's desperation to protect and be loved by her is truly captivating. He caused significant damage, fighting intruders, politicians, and hooligans, ultimately tarnishing the college's reputation.

As she continues reading, she discovers that Anjali had conflicting feelings towards Aryan, with one side of her loving him and the other supporting him like a constant companion. For the first time, she experienced jealousy because Anjali used to share everything, from secrets to belongings, but this time, she wouldn't even drop a hint about Aryan. Anjali cherished the feelings she experienced when he touched her body, describing them as precious.

Divya recalls how he tightly embraced her and asserted his dominance in the manager's office. She closed the diary and took out every portrait of Aryan that Anjali had drawn. As she gazes into each portrait, she becomes captivated by his gaze, his lips, his face, his strength, and she loses herself in their love story. It was Aryan who yearned for Anjali's love with an intense passion.

Divya departed to learn more about them. Standing in front of their cursed home, she entered to find a dark and quiet atmosphere as she made their way through the broken items to their upstairs bedroom. She observed the bed sheet, which was crumpled in an even messier fashion, and then noticed the crumpled note, which was Aryan's last message. Aryan relinquished all his rights to Anjali's company in the contract and she finally received the studio address where his gift was recorded.

Having learned this, she departed from the house and glanced back one last time, contemplating, "I will transform this accursed house into the beautiful place my elder sister desired."

Upon arriving at the studio, she requested a meeting with the owners. At the meeting, she begins by stating, "I am Divya Pandey, the younger sister of Anjali Pandey. Until Anjali returns as the director, I will be assuming the role and all the associated responsibilities. I'm here because of the contract in Aryan Mishra's name—I need it immediately."

Upon saying this, she sent the contract copy, upon seeing which the studio owners stated, "It cannot be released as the rights belong to Aryan Mishra and will remain with him until Anjali Pandey signs the contract."

Divya's lawyer stated that if the former boss experiences mental issues or an accident, all power and shares will be transferred to Divya Pandey, the co-owner. He presented the modified contract to the studio owners, replacing Anjali Pandey's name with Divya Pandey, and everyone unanimously agreed and signed the agreement.

With full rights to Aryan's composition, Divya has prepared everything for its release at the college. Yet, she holds back from spreading it, reminding herself of her commitment to repairing the college's tarnished image caused by Aryan's vindictiveness. The tune aired on the radio and instantly captivated listeners, leading to it becoming a viral sensation and drawing a massive crowd to the college.

Aryan's savage actions tarnished the college's reputation, but Divya managed to restore it through her emotional connection. Everything was going well until chaos erupted at the college. When she glanced at the main ground, she witnessed Aryan Mishra angrily making his way towards the auditorium, brandishing a gun. Divya unlocked the door and silently stood back, waiting for him as she saw him approach.

Divya was confused when he didn't show up after a while, and then she saw the fluid spreading rapidly inside the room. She discovered it was kerosene and, breathing heavily, hurriedly tried to retrieve the CD before escaping. However, before she could do so, she noticed Aryan outside the room who, without hesitation, lit the fire and threw it inside. When he does this, his eyes filled with hatred and a smile on his lips, he finally allows his pain to burn alive.

Divya, witnessing his intense hatred up close for the first time, appears bewildered in that instant as her bodyguards rush to her rescue, safely extracting her from the dangerous situation. Divya attempted to save the copy before her guards forcibly took her, leading to a sudden blast in the auditorium.

The staff and crew worked to escape the fire, but Divya stayed at the site. Once everything was resolved, Divya quickly rushed inside to search for the copy. However, to her dismay, everything had turned to ashes. She was frustrated because Aryan had taken the only piece of evidence that could prove her right, and she was about to leave. However, she pauses when her gaze falls upon the envelope resting on her car's windshield. Upon searching, she found the last copy of Aryan's composition. Holding the CD, she looked around and spotted him leaving quietly, prompting her to leave as well.

3

Chapter Three

The other day,

A massive group of people and journalists assembled at the college, anticipating Aryan's arrival. Divya arrived at the college with the armed forces to calm down the crowd after a while. Divya begins by clarifying that the incident occurred the previous day and assures everyone that no one was harmed, and everything has already been addressed. One person from the crowd asked her if she had the rights for the composition, she released the previous day.

Divya, with the contract in hand, navigates through the bustling crowd, listening to the mix of conversations around her. Upon her arrival, everyone cleared the path for her, and she handed the contract to someone while asserting, "I have complete authority."

Aryan saw the name Divya Shukla, the new college CEO, had claimed rights to his composition. Not expecting it, he shut his eyes while pondering. The college crowd appeared frightened by his tension, and a member of the media asked Divya when the full version of the trending song would be released, which everyone was eagerly waiting for.

Aryan looked helplessly at Divya while she looked back at him. She assured him, "I won't keep the viewers waiting for too long. The full song will be released very soon." Aryan seemed lost upon hearing this and attempted to read the contract, but his eyes were brimming with tears, and he couldn't focus. Aryan was approached by the media for his views, but he stayed silent and then threw away the contract before leaving.

Everyone else left, but Divya stayed and secured the contract. As she looks at it, she reads out her altered name - Divya Shukla. Reflecting on the day that led to her name change, she pondered the reasons and events that had compelled her to make such a sudden alteration before meeting Aryan.

Prior to attending college,

Divya played the recording of the cursed house and saw Aryan entering home from the studio. He noticed Anjali was missing and found a note from her sister saying, "I am taking my sister back."

Upon reading this, he became enraged and started angrily breaking things, eventually cursing the house and issuing a death threat to Anjali's sister if they were to meet again. Before she could even enter his life, she learns of Aryan's deep animosity towards herself. Divya remembers what her mom said about Aryan, "Trust only him. He's got the solution to all our problems, even the ones we don't know yet. Stick with him no matter what."

Remembering what her mom said and thinking about how bad things were for Anjali, Divya decided to change her name and be part of Aryan's life.

Present time,

When Aryan was leaving, Divya asked with a curious tone, "Why did you choose to return the last copy instead of keeping it for yourself if you truly didn't want it to be released?"

After listening, he stopped and said, "I wish I hadn't saved you from that fire because the worst gift of my life is you."

Divya is alone in her villa, sitting on the chair where Anjali used to sit, constantly pondering over his final words to her: "It's the worst gift of his life."

With this thought in mind, she quickly snatched the diary back and continued reading. Divya finally reached a point where Anjali hurt Aryan in the worst way, leading him to curse her with all his heart for the first time, nearly taking her life.

Learning this part of her sister's life, she realized that she wouldn't be able to bear the pain she had endured, as she read about the depth of her suffering. Filled with anger, she slammed the diary shut and spent the entire night tormented by the pain caused by Aryan's hurtful words.

4
Chapter Four

The other day,

Divya sat in the manager's room of the college, contemplating the pain caused by Aryan. Just like her sister, she wants to inflict the same miserable feelings on him, so she immediately asked the college administration to change the rules to suit her desires. She specifically mentioned Aryan Mishra's name to ensure his return to college and resolve the issues he caused. Do whatever it takes to bring him back or else terminate his enrollment.

Despite multiple reminders, Aryan failed to show up, leading to a request for his termination letter. As this occurred, the new manager, who is also the head dean, arrived and publicly tore up the termination letter and contract out of anger, declaring, "He is like a son to me, and he doesn't deserve this."

She seemed astonished and asked him directly, "Why do you care about him so much when everyone hates him for constantly damaging the college's reputation?"

He responded, saying, "He's not how he seems at the moment. He's just a little upset about something he can't explain, but we can all sense it. Every single person in this college loves him because he's unique and his identity will restore everything that he took. However, be assured that he is the most important asset for restoring your college reputation. All he requires is some time and care to recover, and that's all."

With anger in his voice, he sternly instructed the admin to stop issuing any more termination letters for him. As he was about to leave, Divya spoke up, demanding that he be brought back to the college. She wanted to see if he truly lived up to the recommendations before deciding what to do with him.

He heeds her warning and leaves, after which she becomes even more eager to meet Aryan again and continues to wait for him. It's been a couple of days, but he still won't come back to this college. Finally, she decides to go to the administration room herself and issues a termination letter for him. She was heading towards the CEO room when she was abruptly pulled into a dark room and pressed against the wall.

She gazed into his eyes as he admired her from head to toe. She could sense his firm grip around her waist as he remained fixated on her red lips, appearing too close for comfort. He abruptly snatched the termination letter from her grasp and discovered it lacked just one thing to be finalized: her consent. He promptly handed her his pen, insisting she sign the letter immediately, and seeing his determination, she complied instantly.

When she does this, he immediately feels calm and gratefully thanks her, saying, "Thank you for finally relieving me from all the pain this college has brought to my life. You have finally ended my pain by terminating me, and I wholeheartedly bless you. Let this be our final meeting.

She tore the contract in front of him, seeing his fake happiness, and then pushed him against the wall, locking eyes with him. Despite his efforts to conceal everything, she knew all too well that he was still suffering from the pain of their separation, a pain she had inflicted upon him.

By witnessing this, she reached out and touched his heart, enabling her to feel all his lingering pain. Finally, she asked him why he was grateful to her despite her taking his composition, which was originally a gift for someone important to him. Even though I took it from you, and you're hurt, you still thank me wholeheartedly. But why won't you reveal everything to me? Do you not want me to hurt you like someone from your past did, to make you feel alive again?

He took the sharp object and cut his hand, causing it to bleed. She was panicked and tried to stop the bleeding while yelling at him, "Are you crazy? Don't you feel any pain?"

"Yes," he responded, "I was able to feel and was striving to survive until you took away my only source of hope. Since you took it away, I feel nothing, even if you hurt me or do whatever you want. I simply don't feel alive after what you intentionally did to me."

As he said this, he was departing, causing her to feel remorseful for her actions, which were unjust. He cared deeply for her elder sister, and if she were to do the same, she might feel the same way. Wondering about her sister's actions, she suddenly said, "I want you to come back to this college no matter what, and I hope you'll come back to your princess because I'm the only one who can hurt you or care for you the most."

Hearing the same words his girl used to say, he appeared shocked by her knowledge of every detail about him, yet he remained silent and quietly left the college, followed by Divya leaving for her villa. Divya remains seated, fixated on her hand stained with his blood. She remained trapped in feelings of remorse, believing she had treated him poorly. Feeling tense and still pondering what her sister could do after wronging him, she wanted to apologize.

She resumed reading the diary to find out where their story would go. She read the book daily while anticipating his return to college, only to realize he never went back, proving his final words, "may this be our last meeting." She repeatedly recalled the word, then grabbed her phone and instructed her team to immediately reverse the order. Now, she eagerly awaits the outcome, hoping it will bring him back to college.

5

Chapter Five

After 2 weeks,

One day, while Divya was waiting for Aryan, she was shocked to see him standing so close to her as she got out of her luxurious car at college. As she catches sight of him, she immediately feels calm. Before he can even take a single step toward her, her bodyguards become alert, still not trusting him. However, she commands everyone to step back.

Standing alone in front of him, she gazes into his eyes, filled with newfound happiness and a desire to share something he had longed for. Prior to disclosing anything, he presented a flower to her, saying, "Thank you, once more."

Hearing the word again, he smiled instead of getting angry, causing her to ask him, "Isn't this not about expelling you from college?"

As he calmly sits in her car, he slowly pulls her towards him and expresses gratitude for not releasing his composition now or never. My gift, which I nearly lost, is now safely in your hands, and I trust you won't diminish its specialness. I have no desires or words left to ask of you.

Finally, he kissed both her eyes and admitted, "I misjudged you; you're actually my WELL-WISHER."

The way he reveals his desires while respecting her boundaries makes her feel loved and cared for. Experiencing this divine sensation she had only previously read about in the diary; she is now living it firsthand. She feels incredibly special because of the way he cares for her, and she seals it with a kiss on his forehead, promising to fulfill his every wish.

Slowly, she expressed her gratitude that he had returned to her because she needed him desperately. The way she holds him tightly and uses affectionate words makes him uncomfortable, so he slowly pushes her away and leaves. She interpreted his insecurity as a desire to distance himself from her concern, so she asked from behind him, "I'm still not content with your attentiveness—I want even more from you."

Despite hearing the same word again, he appears shocked but remains unresponsive to her words. On his way home, the new college manager stopped him and seemed delighted to see him back. Without saying a word, he immediately embraced him tightly, making him feel like his own son.

Finally, he hugged him back, leaving everyone amazed as he stood still and allowed his dean to hug him even longer. Dean said, "Son, I always believed in you and now that you're back, I want you to stay and show everyone that I was right. Prove the doubters wrong by staying humble and quiet in this college, just like you used to be!"

Aryan appears to be caught in a hypothetical situation, torn between wanting to leave and being unable to do so easily after witnessing his manager's dedication. He made a promise in front of everyone that he would stay here and give his best effort, just as he had hoped for.

As everyone listened, they praised him for putting his dean's pride first, despite his personal issues. Divya finally left the college after witnessing the special moment of seeing Aryan back, the memory etched in her heart. While leaving, she whispered to herself, "From now on, every recording of you will only be about us, marking the beginning of a new story - Aryan Mishra and Divya Pandey."

6

Since that day, she never set foot in the college, while Aryan, on the other hand, continued to come but kept his distance from everyone, remaining in the same state. Though everyone thought he was fine, he was still sinking into a worse state, but he tried to stand up so she wouldn't see him as helpless as before as this would ruin all her hard work to bring him back to life. By watching recordings, she witnesses his ongoing internal battle and resistance towards living freely.

As she learned more about him, she discovered how his lack of sensing her care drove him to insanity, leading him to turn to drugs, become violent towards others, and ultimately inflict self-harm if the pain became unbearable. Divya suddenly panicked upon reading everything about him, realizing she was the one who had done the worst in their life. Initially, she was overprotective of her sister, but as she grew closer to Aryan and understood his loneliness, she became obsessed with him, witnessing his deteriorating state daily.

Aryan, on his usual day, suddenly stops when he notices Anjali's car in the premises. Upon witnessing this, he hurried towards the manager's office. As he entered the dark room, he spotted Anjali standing there. Without hesitation, he held her tightly and confessed, "I missed you so much, Miss Pandey." Then, he kissed her deeply.

While they were doing this, they suddenly heard a knock at the door and someone saying, "Ma'am, we need to leave for a meeting." Upon hearing this, she departed without uttering a word to him. As she was departing, he started sensing something peculiar about her. As he watches her depart, he gently brushes his lips, recalling her essence, which appears to have transformed. When he discovered it wasn't his girlfriend, but her sister, who had come to see him. Filled with frustration, he begins ruthlessly breaking things, unable to bear the sight of her, powerless to take action.

Meanwhile, Divya continued reading the rest of the diary to discover more about Aryan's love and care. For the first time, she experiences jealousy towards her sister and contemplates his unspoken words, unfulfilled desires, and unaccepted care that he always shows her. Wondering why she couldn't be the girl who fulfills all his wishes and heals his wounds, she asked herself this question, "Why can't I be the girl he can hold in his arms when he needs someone the most? Why can't I be the girl he can embrace passionately whenever he desires?"

As she says this, a memory of the meeting in the manager's room today floods back into her mind. She remembers the gentle touch and tender care he showed her, as if he were completely infatuated. She holds herself with love, cherishing this precious feeling that she had never experienced before, being with Aryan.

Divya, who appeared visibly tense, hurried towards the college after a few days. When she arrived, she found the media and followers gathered, all asking for one thing: the release date of his full album.

Seeing all this, she starts walking towards Aryan. He stands still in the middle of the ground, silent and unable to utter a single word. The surroundings serve as painful reminders of his deepest anguish, a pain he continues to conceal. Unable to share or express his grievance, he now appears utterly shattered, consumed by his pain. Standing in front of him, she moved her hand slowly towards his face, her fingertips trembling with tenderness. As she touched his face, she saw his eyes welling up with tears, a reflection of the pain he could no longer bear.

Upon witnessing his state, her patience wore thin, and she immediately commanded her armed forces to disperse the crowd, swiftly clearing the area while forcefully dealing with any opposition, reducing the place to ruins in an instant. In their exclusive world, she allows him to see nothing but her eyes. When everything was finally cleared, he slowly turned his gaze towards the mess she made for him. Upon witnessing this, he shuts his eyes, unwilling to acknowledge the situation, intensifying his self-loathing, as he believes he only brings calamity wherever he goes.

Upon learning this, she attempted to soothe him, but he insisted on bearing the pain alone, as only his girl could truly understand it. Divya, as she was leaving, gently passed a note to his hand, and then he quietly headed towards the library. Seeking relief, he sits alone, reminiscing about the times his girl would come here to find him. He is currently missing her deeply and decides to open the note which Divya gave him that mentions, "If you don't feel my presence around you, then maybe you can sense the warmth of my feelings, which I only reveal to you. I love sharing everything with you because we're alike in our fear of the dark."

Reading the same word he had used to calm the unknown girl who worried about losing him soon left him shocked. He rose and began searching for the book he had placed somewhere in the library. Finally, when he located the precise spot, he carefully retrieved his personal diary where he had almost neglected to reveal anything more about himself after her departure. Experiencing intense pain, he desired to document these emotions solely in his diary, prompting him to open it once more.

While opening it, he noticed something out of the ordinary inside. Instead of starting from the first page, he opted to begin from the back. There, he came across Anjali's heartfelt writing, which he absorbed with his gaze. He struggles to communicate his feelings to her, even though she wrote everything down, expressing how she sees him as unique compared to everyone else.

He quickly shuts the diary upon reading the phrase "unique friend," not wanting to experience any more pain. He then exits the college grounds, while Divya, standing at a distance, watches him until he disappears.

7
Chapter Seven

After few days,

Aryan rushes angrily towards a specific location. He reaches there and stands in front of Divya at the meeting. The only thing everyone asks about is the release date of the album they invested in. They have already completed their promotion, but now they face charges of fraud with viewers, and they won't rest until she returns the composition.

As they all yelled and questioned her, he stepped in and declared, "It's my composition and no one has the right to question it. If anyone does, I will destroy everything as if there was nothing worth fighting for here."

They all appeared terrified and pleaded, "We need a way to protect ourselves. We can't end up in prison because of her. We trusted her, but now she refuses to give us the album. If it doesn't get released, we'll all go to jail."

He falls silent for a moment while listening to the facts. He requested them to draft a new contract that includes the statement, "I, Aryan Mishra, am willingly creating 3 songs for the same company. If I don't deliver an alternative to my first composition within a month, I will be solely responsible for all charges and petitions, as the company shareholders are not involved. Aryan Mishra should be solely responsible for all charges and damages faced by the company now or in the future."

He stood in front of the crew, shocking them as he prepared to take responsibility for all the damage done in Divya's name. She remained at his back, unwilling to accept the proposal and struggling to navigate this situation. After a while, a new contract was presented to him. With just one glance, he instinctively grabbed a pen and signed it without hesitation. Suddenly, he feels her hand gently clutching his own, her touch filled with fear and desperation to keep their promise intact. Recognizing her insecurity, he quickly signed the contract and assumed full responsibility, earning praise from everyone before they all left with a new contract to deliver to their CEO.

Gradually, he looks towards her, seeing her tear-filled eyes, making her feel guilty. As he attempted to wipe away her tears, she clung to him tightly, breaking down in tears because she desperately didn't want this to happen. He is now uncertain about how to interact with her. With gentle tenderness, he pressed his lips against her forehead, then moved to her tear-filled eyes, softly kissing them. He whispered, "Your prestige means everything to me; it's you who holds my deepest care."

Feeling low, she couldn't bear to stay in that place any longer, especially being so close to him. Despite his pain, he continued to put on a facade of being alright. As she gets off from him, she turns to leave but pauses for a moment to confront him, her voice dripping with contempt, "You are still a hypocrite?"

Divya went straight to the college library, searching for something valuable. When she couldn't find it, she realized he had taken the diary with him. After learning this, she appears confused and begins destroying things without mercy, desperate to get the diary back. All her deepest emotions were carefully recorded in his diary, safely guarded until he finally took it. She felt completely lost, unsure of when she would ever regain her emotions. This made her worry that Aryan might mistake her detachment for her sister's, but deep down, she also had her own hidden feelings that she refused to share with anyone.

In a state of helplessness, she settled herself on the ground. Aryan handed her the diary, saying that it used to belong to him but now it's a curse, yet he trusts her to keep it safe like she kept his gift safe. "I don't want to destroy the feelings someone else has poured into this diary, but if I keep it close, it might get ruined." said Aryan.

As a promise, she gently retrieved his diary from his grasp, ensuring their emotions would remain safe. Divya, after regaining her precious feelings, leaves for her villa, feeling calm, while he appears serene.

Aryan is now alone in the library, contemplating the contract he signed to protect his precious gift. However, he is unsure how to resolve the issue without Anjali.

8

Chapter Eight

Divya sits calmly while her crew members, standing in front, are chained by her armed forces. Begging before her, they plead, "We've completed all your requests. He signed the contract as you desired. Please spare us, we'll do anything you ask."

Upon hearing this, she angrily kicked the table and moved towards them, grabbing the person by the collar and shouting, "I only asked you to get him to sign the contract, but you exceeded the set limit three times without my permission. Whose idea was this?"

All others retreat, leaving only the person she was gripping by the collar. Upon understanding this, she instructed the release of all the prisoners and distributing their shares, along with their advance profits. She requested, "Now you all need to put pressure on him to finish the work as soon as possible."

With a sudden gesture, she aims the gun at them and issues a warning, "Follow my commands exactly, and anyone who exceeds them will face destruction this time, I swear. If I witness him suffering due to any of your terrible choices, please remember my humble warning before embarking on anything new."

In response to the warning, they silently make their exit. Alone, she gazes at the contract and then at his signature, placed just behind hers, which she adores. She hurts him to the worst to achieve her dominance, then triumphantly takes what she desired and gently holds her sister's diary, asking for apology, "I'm sorry for making him fulfill your dreams. Until you return to our lives in good health, I promise to care for him as you always did. The gift I have for him may hurt now, but in the future, he will be praised for the work and effort invested in him. I promise to make your dream, which you've seen with open eyes, a reality. You are the only one deserving of his affection, and if it's not you, then he doesn't want anyone else's care. I tried to win his attention, but I felt nothing because his heart belongs solely to you and no one else."

With tears in her eyes, she goes straight to her room and isolates herself to bear the pain alone. Once again, she attempted to capture this feeling of herself in Aryan's diary, hoping to escape the current overwhelming emotions.

9

Chapter Nine

After few days,

Divya, feeling tense, quickly makes her way to college. Upon arrival, she noticed that everyone appeared terrified, and nobody attempted to enter the music room. Witnessing this, she commanded her men to disperse the crowd before attempting to enter the room herself. She saw Aryan sitting all alone. She navigates through the shattered musical equipment and kneels, clutching Aryan's bleeding hand. By gently touching his face and making him look at her, she instilled the belief that he can accomplish anything with just a little support.

When he sees Divya, he recalls Anjali's words about always being there for him when he's hurt or in need, so he embraces her tightly. Witnessing his current state, she is overwhelmed with guilt, as her intention was only to fulfill her sister's wish. However, in the process, she continues to hurt him repeatedly, and now she can't undo it since he willingly signed the contract to save her, the source of his suffering.

Witnessing his vulnerability, she guides him to the college garden while holding his hand. Slowly, she let go of his hand as she continued towards the piano under the big tree. Serenely seated, she began playing the exquisite melody, surpassing even Aryan's tune in beauty. Upon hearing this, he walks over to her and sits beside her, focusing solely on her notes as she plays the tune, which gradually brings him a sense of calm.

She consistently plays new, beautiful tunes every day, which he listens to carefully, trying to learn the notes and melodies that only she can play so beautifully, even better than he ever could. Now, he comes to college to find her, hoping she'll listen to his precious tune, but always leaves quietly, oblivious to the feelings she's tried to express.

As usual, when Aryan was about to leave after hearing her melody, Divya asked from behind, "Will you stay longer?"

As he listens, he gradually moves closer to her and sits by her side, admiring her ornaments and dress. He admires her from all angles but avoids eye contact as if he doesn't want her to know more about him. "I feel lost when I see you in pain," Divya said, her voice filled with empathy.

The moment she speaks, he falls into a hushed silence, as if unable to find the right words to answer her question. Being tense, he abruptly stood up and started to walk away. From behind him, she asked, "I know this brings back painful memories for you, but from now on, everything you do belongs to me. It will bring you peace and relieve your pain."

As she walked close to him, he could feel her presence, and finally, she confessed, "I feel a sense of uniqueness when I'm near you."

She starts to reveal a small part of herself, ready to return his diary, but he quickly departs without a glance or reclaiming it. As he walked away from her, she captured his departure in her eyes, unwilling to acknowledge or express the feeling of abandonment after her attempts to reveal her ignored feelings.

She left that place soon after he did, and neither of them returned to college after that day. Aryan, who was running out of time, ignored his feelings of loneliness and loss until one day when he decided to run towards college in search of something valuable. Upon arrival, he heads straight to the music room only to find it locked, just as it has been since that day. He searched everywhere for her but couldn't find a trace of her.

While searching for her, Aryan received a mysterious call and immediately rushed to the specified location. When he arrived, he noticed a crew member waiting for him. With anticipation in his voice, he asked a single question: "When will our composition be released? We're eagerly awaiting its unveiling, as it will also signal our liberation from this contract."

As he listens, he scans the surroundings in search of one. Unable to spot her, he quietly sat down and began writing in front of them. Observing his peculiar actions, they patiently wait for him. Once he finished, he picked up a few more papers and, after he was done writing, he moved all of them to the crew's side. When they saw the three new composition lyrics at once, they were all filled with awe and immediately wanted to copyright them. Aryan took out the other contract, observing their excitement. As they all read it, their expressions shifted from excitement to shock, leaving them unsure of what to do next.

Aryan informed everyone that there is a rival company eagerly waiting to sign a contract with him, and they will also remove all charges and upcoming petitions against him. They all seemed tense after hearing this and asked him what he really wanted from them.

"Divya Shukla," he replied, his voice filled with emotions. "Bring her back to me, without her, this composition remains incomplete. She is the soul that breathes life into these words. You all have a strict deadline of three days to retrieve her, and during this time, our contract remains valid; otherwise, I will obliterate everything when the deadline expires."

Aryan leaves, giving them all a time limit, and now waits patiently. He had been silent for nearly three days, with no updates from the crew. He waited anxiously in the same music room where he had last seen her. After being there for three days without any rest, he felt a wave of dizziness wash over him as he spotted Divya standing before him. As he saw her approaching, he fell into a hushed silence, his gaze fixed on her as if he needed reassurance of her existence. To confirm his suspicions, he gently reached out and clasped her hand. As he held her hand, he whispered, "It took three long days for my emotions to return."

In response, she said, "You only prioritize your emotions, leaving no room for me. I feel like I have no identity except being a caretaker for you." Noticing his silence, she felt the sudden urge to leave, but then she froze upon hearing a peculiar sound. When she turned back, she was startled to find Aryan unconscious. Holding him close to her heart, a wave of guilt washes over her for leaving him alone, his grip on her hands tightening to stay close.

10

Chapter Ten

After 2 days,

Upon returning to college, Aryan discovered that all his work, projects, and routines had already been completed, causing him to head towards the library. However, to his dismay, he found everything in a state of disarray. While setting up the place, meticulously organizing each item, he abruptly halted when he caught sight of his diary, unexpectedly positioned in the exact same slot. Clutching his diary tightly, he made a conscious effort to confront his past instead of running away from it. He whispered to himself, "I know this brings back painful memories for you, but from this moment forward, I will take control. I promise you, there will be peace and no more suffering."

With these thoughts in mind, he eagerly opens the diary and begins reading. There, he finds her heartfelt words describing how she sees him as someone distinct from everyone else and the depth of her care for him. Aryan, who read everything, finally got to the part where she openly asks him, "Can I have some of your care?"

As he reads this, he promptly closes the diary. Divya, who poured her heart out in her diary, always sought solace in its pages. However, one day, she discovered it was gone, and panic set in as she searched frantically in every nook and cranny. Seeing her tense, Aryan stood on her back and slowly handed the diary back to her. As she turned to leave, he asked, "Can I have a bit of your care for myself?"

The moment he asked her, she immediately wrapped her arms around him, finding solace in his embrace after a prolonged period of uncertainty, not wanting to lose him now. He asked her, "Please forgive me because I don't want to lose anyone who cares for me so deeply."

As she listened, her eyes welled up with tears, prompting him to hold her even closer to his heart. It feels as if she is perpetually apologizing to him, concealing something she doesn't want to confront, and it's like a dream when Aryan directly asks for her attention.

After holding him tight for a while, she mustered up the courage to speak, her voice trembling as she said, "I want to be your well-wisher, just like you once asked me. I want to be your shadow, always there to guide you through the darkness when you feel lost. I want to be the person who will cherish and look after you with unwavering devotion. I want to be there for you in all your hardships, willing to listen and support you without expecting anything in return. All I ask for is a small place in your heart where I can be open with you whenever you need me."

Her fear lingered, but she couldn't contain her emotions any longer. With a trembling voice, she confessed, "I might not be the girl you remember, but being with you makes me feel unique. Even though I am aware of your past and your unique friend, your eyes reveal the shattered pieces of your heart, which I am determined to heal with my nurturing love."

As he listened intently, he gently kissed her eyes, expressing his desire for her to be his lifelong supporter. As a token of thanks, he handed her a small gift, a gesture that spoke volumes.

11

Chapter Eleven

Later at that night,

Slowly unwrapping the packed gift, she couldn't help but recall the incident that occurred in college earlier today. She keeps on repeating the same line, her voice filled with longing, "I want you to be my well-wisher for life." She couldn't fathom that he wouldn't abandon her until he convinced her of his unwavering commitment.

She eagerly unpacked the little gift and her eyes widened at the sight of a delicious cake and an assortment of cookies. As she bit into it, the flavors of his handmade cookie exploded in her mouth. She cherishes his innocent present, knowing she cannot protect it, but his heartfelt gesture will forever reside in her heart as the most precious gift she had ever received.

Divya's infatuation with Aryan gradually blossomed into genuine love. As she mustered the courage to admit her feelings, she found herself passing through the living room. Her gaze was drawn to her mother's favorite chair, where Anjali had spent countless hours during her most difficult moments of illness.

Divya's heart sank as she recalled the harrowing moment when her sister teetered on the brink of death.

Flashback starts

Divya quickly packed her belongings and finally took Anjali's phone, her fingers trembling as she sent a desperate text to Aryan:

"I need you, please help me."

Aryan seemed tense as he hastily left his house, but then he spotted his sister and urgently requested her to take care of the family in his absence. Reaching there, he pauses for a moment before the gate, taking in the familiar sights and sounds. He retrieves the key he always carries and unlocks the gate, his mind filled with memories of the incident that had caused him to be separated from Anjali. A wave of fear washes over him, wondering what state she might be in now.

Deep in thought, he absentmindedly grasped the gate's handle, not realizing it had been unlocked from the very beginning. As he entered the house, he could hear the creaking of the floorboards beneath his feet. Moving closer to her, he finally whispered, "Anjali."

As she turned to his side, he finally saw her in a pitiful state, unable to stand and on the verge of collapsing. Holding her breath, he asked with tension in his voice, "Anjali, what has happened to you? Don't worry, I'm here with you, just keep your eyes locked on mine."

She whispered, tears streaming down her face, "My mother left me all alone in this world. What were her final words to you?"

She looked at him with a shocked expression, his silence speaking volumes. Annoyed, she asked him again, "What did she tell you in her final moments?"

As he saw her losing her patience and enduring pain, he held her tighter, trying to bring her calmness, while she persistently asked the same question. As he remained silent, she couldn't resist inflicting pain upon him, even as she clung to him, longing to uncover her mother's last words. "Just tell me," She pleaded, "what were her final words?"

Seeing her lost, he then finally answered, his voice filled with conviction, "She wants us to be together forever, never to part after this!" As she listened, her heart broke and tears welled up in her eyes, causing her to hold him even tighter.

Divya, who was observing them from a distance, appeared emotional, as her sister finally seemed at peace after a long period of unrest. As she looked at them, a sense of relief washed over her, knowing that only Aryan had the power to revive her. With that thought in mind, she left.

At present,

As she reminisced about the past, her love for Aryan, which had been blossoming from her broken heart, vanished. She gently placed the handmade dish that Aryan had made beside Anjali's chair. She realized that everything in that place reminded her of Aryan, her sister was the only comfort she had left, and with tears streaming down her face, she left and retreated to her room.

12

Chapter Twelve

Aryan, going about his normal tasks in college, always has the eerie sensation of being followed. One day, unable to shake off the feeling any longer, he grabs the person following him from behind, only to discover that it's Divya. "Tell me," He asked, "why are you always avoiding me now?"

She responded, "I am not the one who continues to pursue a lost soul, the one you love to refer to as Miss Pandey, isn't that her name? I will always stay by your side, but your anger is what frightens me the most."

As he listened, he slowly withdrew his hand, his face filled with disbelief. "I was happy to see you after a long time, but I never expected this from you. I hope you have a hidden agenda for this, so I'm not angry with you. However, I kindly ask you to stay away from me for a while." and left.

The next day,

Aryan finished attending his lecture and made his way to the library. Suddenly, Divya appeared in front of him, but he continued walking, ignoring her. She couldn't help but ask, "Are you still mad at me?"

As he tried to leave, she held his hand, causing him to abruptly turn and ask her, "Aren't you scared of me now?"

As he keeps looking into her eyes, she remains silent, her thoughts hidden behind a calm facade. "I know you won't reveal anything about yourself so easily," she said with a determined look in her eyes. "But I hold a key to your past, and until I have it, you won't be able to shake me off so easily." Saying this, she left. The tension from recent events weighs heavily on him, especially when she constantly reminds him of his painful past. Unable to bear it any longer, he leaves without hesitation.

Despite isolating himself for a few days, he still couldn't find peace, haunted by his past. Feeling tense, he began walking aimlessly, trying to distance himself from everyone. Eventually, he found himself at the park where he used to seek solace, but now he lacked the courage to venture in alone.

Slowly, he turns his gaze to the other side, where his cursed house looms before him. As he entered the house, he locked the door behind him and slowly made his way to his bed. Despite his surroundings, he couldn't shake off the restlessness that still lingered within him. Eventually, he reached for the medicine for anxiety and depression that sat near his bedside, without a prescription. Desperate for some relief, he took a heavy dose and hoped it would bring him some much-needed rest.

It's been almost 2 days since Aryan went missing, and Divya anxiously waits for any news about where he disappeared so suddenly.

Consumed by fear, she ordered a larger group of her men to join in the search for him. She keeps thinking, puzzled by the fact that neither his relatives nor his family had any knowledge of him. If not for them, then who could possibly know where he could have disappeared too so suddenly? I hope he remains out of harm's way.

Frustrated by the lack of information about him, she recalled a line from his diary: "whenever I don't feel calm, I have my special place where I find peace." With this in mind, she veered her car towards the park. Upon arrival, she could still feel the lingering presence of their memories, trapped within the surroundings. After spending some time there, she finally asked herself, "Why can't I find you anywhere? Is there something bothering you? Why haven't you reached out to me, your well-wisher?"

As she turned around, her eyes landed on her sister's cursed house. She reached for the gate, her fingers grazing the cold metal, but she couldn't as it belonged to someone else whom she didn't want to disturb. As she was leaving, she noticed that the gate was already unlocked, so she walked inside and made her way to their room.

As she approached, she saw Aryan lying unconscious amidst a chaotic scene. Upon seeing this, she urgently called out for help, rallying her team to swiftly rush him to the hospital. After thoroughly examining him, the doctor concluded that he was heavily medicated, but his mental faculties and immune system were functioning normally. However, he was diagnosed with severe depression that required immediate treatment to prevent further mental health issues.

When Aryan regained consciousness, he saw himself lying on a hospital bed with a needle in his arm, receiving medication. While everyone else was resting, he continued to walk towards the hospital door. Just as he was about to leave, he found himself surrounded by Divya's men, determined to prevent his escape. Seeing them in opposition, he lost control and turned savage, launching a relentless attack on everyone around him.

In an instant, her men came to a halt, their eyes fixed on Divya as she stood before them, attempting to bring a sense of calm. Aryan then gave her permission to come closer, and without hesitation, she wrapped her arms around him, the only person he truly trusts. Holding him gently, she whispered, "It's just you and me, no one else. Tell me your desired destination, and I'll ensure we go there without anyone trailing behind."

Listening to this, he starts walking, and Divya follows, eventually reaching the same place in the park where they now stand calmly. She admires Aryan for his efforts to find patience, but he still can't enter the park. As she saw his condition worsening, she reached out and grasped his hand, guiding him towards his cursed house. Aryan was now at rest, with Divya seated beside him. As she started feeling dizzy, she carefully lay down next to him, never taking her eyes off his face.

Aryan's grip tightened around her hand, pulling her closer as fear clouded his expression. As she found herself in his embrace, memories of the past flooded back to Divya. She recalled the times when she used to care for Aryan, comforting him as he listened to news about her late mother. Now, in this moment, the situation was familiar, yet the emotions had transformed from care to love.

Divya, being in his arms, couldn't help but admire his strength as he held her tightly, feeling his unspoken desires and the fear that she would never be able to escape his grasp. As she leaned in, her lips brushed against his forehead, leaving a tender kiss behind, and she whispered, "I will restore everything for you, just like it used to be."

13
Chapter Thirteen

Next day,

Slowly waking up from oversleeping, Divya found herself in the same spot where she first saw Aryan, who was still peacefully asleep. As she looked down, she noticed the note she had left for him, lying on the table. Taking it from his side, she noticed that the note was all torn, eliciting a smile from her. "You hate me so much that you won't even try to look at the backside. I clearly mentioned the hospital address where Anjali was admitted, but consumed by your hatred, you failed to read the full note. Now, you unknowingly spent your last night with the person you despise the most, unknowingly giving her the best moment of her life."

She then instructed her men to replace every item in the house with brand new furnishings, and just as they were finishing up, the doctor arrived for a checkup. Noting that he appeared to be in good condition the night before, he provided her with an extended list of medications and then departed. Everything had been set up exactly as she had requested, and now she sat beside him, listening intently for any sign of his consciousness returning. But he remained still and unresponsive. Seeing this, she attempts to assess his nerves.

As soon as she touched him, he jolted awake, tightly gripping her hand, his senses instantly alert. Speaking slowly, her voice trembled as she reassured, "I am here to protect you, please try to calm down." Being drugged heavily, everything appeared blurry before his eyes, but he could still sense her presence and feel the pain he was causing her. As he slowly lost his grip on her hand, he laid back on the bed.

When Aryan finally regained consciousness in the afternoon, he glanced around and spotted Divya patiently waiting for him. Seeing her close, he then asked, "why is it always like this? I always ask for one person's presence around me, but instead of her, I see you standing here. Whenever I feel low or stuck with any trouble, you have always been there to take care of me. Is this our destiny, which I am reluctant to accept, or is it part of your intricate plan?"

As she listened to his words, she felt a sense of rejection and realized she no longer belonged in his life. Without even glancing back at him, she was walking away. As she was about to open the door, she heard a sudden noise coming from his room. Curious, she hurried towards it and found him with a wounded hand, his room in disarray once again.

Seeing him, she seemed scared, unsure if he would remember the last night they had spent together in his bed. As she attempted to approach him, he quickly warned her, "Don't come any closer. I don't want you to witness the darker side of me, filled with nothing but hatred and pain."

Divya paused, her voice filled with regret as she admitted, "I was the one who entered your life, aware of your past and your love for Anjali. But I never intended to come between you two. I always wished to support you, and finally, I willingly became your well-wisher, vowing to never leave your side. As she was leaving, she could hear his silence, which spoke volumes. Suddenly, he tightly grasped her hand, causing her to halt and wince in pain. With a calm voice, she questioned him, "What do you want from me? You won't let me tend to your wounds, yet you refuse to let me leave?"

He replied with a heavy sigh, "My life already feels like a never-ending darkness where I can no longer find solace. If you stay by my side, I fear I might unintentionally cause you harm. Just leave me alone, I don't want you to see my dark side."

Her words were firm as she replied, "I am not scared of you anymore."

She admires him for his intense desire to possess her, and she knows she can no longer suppress her feelings for him when she catches herself biting her lip. In that moment, he abruptly grabs her by the neck and asks, "You crave my darker side, don't you?"

Even though she watched him go wild, she didn't hesitate, anticipating what he would do to her next. Slowly inching closer to him, she whispered, "I want you, and only you. Whether you treat me with tenderness or unleash your wild side, it doesn't matter to me. You are my everything, and I will always be your well-wisher."

As he listened to her words, she felt the tension in his grip on her neck loosen, and he tenderly kissed her neck, whispering, "Please don't leave me alone after this. I can't navigate the darkness on my own anymore." She leaned in and pressed her lips against his, but he remained unresponsive to her affectionate gesture. As she looked at his side, she noticed his unconscious state, prompting her to carefully help him lie on the bed. Just as she was about to leave, a thought stopped her in her tracks thinking, "He pleaded with her not to leave him, even after I poured my heart out to him." and she couldn't help but lie beside him to comfort him.

At the dawn,

Everything seemed fine until Aryan's heartbeat quickened and his body temperature dropped, signaling something was amiss. Divya immediately woke up, attempting to soothe him, but his body seemed uncontrollable. Filled with tension, she administered drugs to him, causing his senses to fade away. Then, she slowly guided him onto herself, relinquishing control and allowing him to explore his desires while making love to her.

In that moment, Aryan appeared consumed, pulling her closer as he showered her body with desperate kisses, treating her with an aggressive passion. She willingly surrendered herself, fulfilling his wild desires, both of them devoid of any opposition. As time ticked by, his longing for her grew wild, while she seemed to lose herself in his commands, willingly fulfilling his every wish.

They had been lying on the same bed for a long time, their love for each other never wavering. Finally, as he lay there calm and at rest, she knew their bond was unbreakable. Divya, who can't help but feel loved for Aryan, still holds onto him tightly. As she kissed his forehead, she made a heartfelt promise. "I vow to never interfere in your life, but to always be a supportive presence, like a well-wisher."

14

Chapter Forteen

After few weeks,

Aryan, having been cured, appears serene and collected in all circumstances. He seemed silent, his footsteps barely making a sound. He no longer showed any signs of fear as he confidently walked through the dark. Sitting alone with his loneliness, he often struggled to recall the details of the past few weeks, which seemed to elude his memory. He only caught brief glimpses of Divya, who seemed to draw closer to him during his recovery, intensifying his determination to solve this mystery.

Whenever she visited him at his park side house, he would always greet her with a quiet smile. She slowly began to recount all the forgotten moments that he couldn't recall, as if they were patiently awaiting her every visit, eager to reveal something new about his past. Just as she had once declared, "I hold a key to your past."

Later at night,

Being lonely in his new house, he always remembers the echo of his last words to Divya, pleading with her not to leave him alone in the darkness he now fears. He glanced at the clock, his eyes moving slowly, before making his way towards the gate and opening the door in one swift motion, greeting his well-wisher who was just about to ring the bell. With a warm smile, he extended his hand and said, "I was waiting for you only, please come in."

She– It's a strange, yet oddly endearing thing about you - I'm still curious to know how you found out that I was here.

He– Whenever you're around me, I can sense your presence as if it's a gentle touch on my skin.

Saying this, he gently clasps her hand and leads her to the dining table, where a delicious spread of food awaits. After dinner, they settled down in the living area, where she entertained him with a series of events that left him amazed and occasionally embarrassed. However, she relished every moment of it.

Aryan sat calmly, listening intently as she spoke. The way she delivered the story, focusing solely on him, made him feel a deep sense of connection. As he pondered this, he glanced at the clock and realized it was nearly midnight. With a sudden burst of courage, he asked her to stay for the night. As she rested, he walked towards her, his mind consumed by the same question. Finally, he couldn't resist asking, "How did you discover this place and find me here when I was unwell?"

She – "I possess a wealth of knowledge about you that surpasses your own understanding. When I sensed your distress, I abandoned everything and tirelessly searched for you until I discovered you lying here unconscious."

Upon hearing this, he asked again, "Do you not feel scared when you stay by my side while taking care of me?"

She - "I never wanted to run away nor hide; all I desired was to be there for you in moments of loneliness."

Upon hearing this, he immediately stood up and prepared to leave, offering his assistance, "I'll be staying in the hall, feel free to call me if you need anything."

"Seems like you haven't slept in days," she said, concern evident in her voice. "I know it must be difficult for you to be alone in the dark. If you want a peaceful sleep, feel free to come to me. I can share my bed and everything with you."

Hearing this, he finds a chair and settles into the room where she is resting. Aryan, who diligently completes all his tasks with a calm demeanor, finally wraps up his work. As he turns to the other side, he notices Divya patiently waiting for him. Aryan carefully guides her to lie down on the bed, studying her dull eyes that long for nothing but his tender care. Being dizzy, he then lies beside her, feeling the world spin around him until his senses gradually settle.

45

15
Chapter Fifteen

On the next day,

As Divya slowly awakened from her sleep, she noticed Aryan tenderly holding her, peacefully asleep. She murmured, "I wonder why you struggle to sleep at night, always needing someone by your side to take care of you. It seems like your impatience with being alone in this house always drives me to come searching for you. Finally, I wish I could freeze this moment with you, lying beside me on this bed."

Filled with love, she gently planted a kiss on his neck. Sensing her presence, Aryan slowly regained consciousness, realizing he was tenderly holding her while she continued to rest peacefully. Seeing this, he tried not to make a sound as he watched her slowly awaken from her sleep. Aryan stood there, silent and motionless, trying not to disrupt her. Seeing his carefulness, she couldn't help but remark, "I always thought you never slept, but here you are, lying next to me. It's quite beautiful, isn't it?"

After getting out of bed, he took a refreshing shower and then made his way to college.

At the college,

After completing his lecture, Aryan proceeded with his usual routines and work, only to find that someone else had taken care of all his tasks in his absence. He seemed amazed as he witnessed the sight and eagerly made his way towards the library. Upon arrival, he found someone diligently arranging books on the shelves. As he put his stuff on the desk, he gently held her hand, causing her to turn around. To his surprise, it was Divya, who appeared visibly angry before quickly resuming her work. Soon, Dean appeared, searching for the CEO. He found her diligently working. He then questioned, "Miss, it's not your responsibility. We have assigned a librarian to handle this task. He will take care of everything."

Upon hearing this, she appeared irritated and retorted, "Don't forget, the librarian is a human being, so use his name when you talk about him. and I love to do whatever work I feel like, especially if it's related to him."

Hearing this, all the college staff quickly departed, leaving them alone. Aryan, visibly stunned, expresses his gratitude to her, saying, "I am truly thankful for everything you have done for me in the past few days."

As he said this, he turned to leave. Suddenly, his body is seized, forcing him to stand against the wall. There, she calmly grabs his collar and locks eyes with him, silently demanding an explanation for what he didn't give her. As he read through her eyes, he gently kissed her forehead, expressing gratitude for everything and apologizing for leaving her alone in the house without a farewell.

"May you have a day filled with joy and blessings, my well-wisher."

With his wishes finally granted, she felt a sense of tranquility settle over her as she departed with a contented smile, ready to embrace the day. Seeing her happy, he was suddenly reminded of his own family, whom he had almost forgotten. With thoughts of them swirling in his mind, he began walking.

Reaching his house, his mother's tear-filled eyes welcomed him with a tight embrace, followed by his sister joining in. Finally reunited with his family, a sense of calm washed over him. As he met his silent father, his eyes spoke volumes, always waiting for his return. After spending a few days with his family, Aryan was preparing to leave again. But before he could go, his mother lovingly packed handmade dishes for Anjali.

"It's been so long since I last saw her," she said. "But you promised to bring her to this house. Until then, I'll let you live alone, knowing that there's someone who will take care of you. Moreover, she needs you by her side, and this thought weighs heavily on me, urging me to ensure your well-being. However, promise me that once she recovers, you will bring her back to this house."

He holds her mother tightly, assuring that he will come back soon. As he was leaving, he noticed his parents and sister coming to see him off. Observing this, he pondered, "To my parents, their world feels incomplete without their children. Their family and children are their cherished treasure, which they obtained through love and countless sacrifices."

As he thought about the promise he had made earlier, a heavy guilt settled in his chest. He reflected on how he had deceived everyone, including his own mother and sister. They all anxiously wait for her, deceived by his lies, hoping for her return to their intertwined lives. The uncertainty of when or if she will come back casts a shadow on their love story.

16

Chapter Sixteen

He reached the entrance of the same park, flooded with memories of every moment he shared with Anjali. But now, he couldn't muster the courage to step inside alone. Fear crept over him in this place, as though the trees, river, and grasses were sentient beings, ready to inquire about her well-being; questioning why he hadn't brought her with him.

As he waits for her return, he contemplates his response to her inevitable question: "What were you doing all these days? Why didn't you come after me when my sister took me away from you? What was holding you back from chasing after me? Don't you possess a heart that yearns to pulsate with the rhythm of my love?"

Standing there for what felt like an eternity, he lost track of whether it was day or night. To escape reality, he closed his eyes, shutting out the world. As he tried to escape, he felt a firm grip on his hand, and a voice asked, "Are you okay, Aryan?"

Without seeing her face, he said, "I don't have the courage to face her when she returns to me, wondering what I did to bring her back. I feel like she slipped through my fingers, gone forever."

As she saw his distress, she immediately embraced him, as he pleaded, "Please, just get me out of here. You always claimed to possess the key to my past. If you have any information about her current whereabouts, please share it with me. I can no longer deceive my family or my conscience."

Kissing his forehead with care she said, "I am here with you and will fix everything for you."

With her steady support, she guided him away from that place towards his house, step by step. Once they arrived, she made him lie down and he immediately began begging for the drug to ease his suffering. Witnessing his deteriorated condition, she administered a potent dose to numb his senses. Standing there, she watches him intently, sensing his unease that refuses to settle. In the presence of his helplessness, she couldn't resist undressing herself, her thoughts drifting back to that unforgettable night that was about to be relived, all while keeping him completely unaware.

With this, she gently pressed her lips against his, savoring the sweetness of their connection. She seemed desperate to relive that night again with him, yearning for the feel of their bodies intertwined in the same bed. In the wild moments on the bed, he made her feel like the center of his universe, fulfilling every desire with an intensity that left her breathless.

Divya had been awake for a long time while Aryan was still asleep. She couldn't sleep and continued to gaze at him, wondering why he always forgot that she loved him deeply, even though he constantly broke her heart by reminding her that they could never be together. She said, "my sister's description of your was so captivating that it made my heart flutter with love. But despite my devotion and care for you, you continuously reject my feelings. You prevent anything that could bring us closer together, constantly reminding me of my sister, for whom you still long to have back in your life. With tears in her eyes, she hugged him tightly, fearing the day she would lose him once her sister returned to their lives."

17
Chapter Seventeen

On the next day,

When Divya woke up, she saw Aryan lying next to her, still peacefully asleep. She cautiously attempted to slip away before he woke up, but he gently held onto her, not wanting to let her go. Even after spending the whole night together, he still yearned for more of her presence. She carefully slipped away from his side, making sure not to disturb his peaceful slumber and keeping their shared secret from the night before hidden.

After some time, when Aryan woke up, he felt a pounding headache and his stomach growled with hunger. As he heard the voice coming from the kitchen, he descended the stairs, curious about who else was present. He was amazed watching Divya prepare the food, but suddenly he held her back, causing her to scream as if she had been hurt by his touch. He grabbed her hand and asked, "Are you injured? What happened?"

She appeared fine as she turned, then asked him, "Did you sleep well last night?" "In a casual tone, he mentioned that he can hardly recall anything. However, whenever he tries to remember, he sees something strange and wonders if it's real. He then asked, 'So, what happened last night?'"

Without hesitation, she tells him the truth, saying, "Tell me where to begin because once I bring you here, you won't let me go, thinking I was your girl. Despite being hurt, you showed me care and shared your pain with me. This time, I don't want to share this feeling with anyone, not even with you."

She indirectly dropped a hint to him by saying this. Upon hearing this, Aryan reached out and gently grasped her hand, expressing his gratitude. "Thank you for taking care of me. Without you, I would have stumbled a long time ago. I know I may not have much influence over you, nor have I given you anything valuable, but I still hope you'll be there for me whenever I need assistance."

Listening to his words, she immediately reached out and embraced him, whispering, "You've already given me the most priceless memories."

While she was resting at night, Aryan silently entered her room and took his diary. As he gazed at her peaceful sleep, he yearned to preserve the image forever. With anticipation, he opened his diary, only to find that his previous note, where he had vividly depicted her, was nowhere to be found. Noticing its absence, he begins to search everywhere, desperately hoping to find it. He settled onto the bed, choosing to face away, and sometime later, he caught a glimpse of a note being surreptitiously passed to him by Divya saying, "I've already read about every feeling of Anjali and yours, but this one doesn't seem to belong to her. It feels more personal, like it's connected to me. Before I delve into it, I just want to confirm with you."

Without facing her, he whispered, "You can read it, but if you sense any unease, please avoid looking at me afterwards." Divya began reading the words he had written, and she could feel all the emotions he had poured into describing her and the way he felt whenever they were near. After reading it all, she was at a loss for words and unsure how to react. Without saying anything else, she abruptly left him alone in that room.

18

Chapter Eighteen

Next day,

Aryan, when trying to enter the college, finds himself barred from accessing any area, whether it be his lecture hall, workplace, or the library. He feels trapped and isolated. Finally, he made his way to the CEO room, finding it unlocked and ready for him. As he entered, he saw Divya waiting for him. In response, she calmly echoed his words, "If you sense something amiss, you are free to abandon me."

The more he listened to her, the clearer it became why she was doing all this. Drawing nearer, she spoke softly, wanting to convey the emotions that had been awakened within her after reading his note. "I don't want to put on a false persona to please you; I simply want you to embrace me for who I truly am, just as I have accepted you as you are. Now, either shower me with love or unleash your wild side, but I want you by my side, close and intimate." As she inched closer, she finally admitted, "Your feelings are the reason I am the way I am now."

Before he could comprehend anything, she kissed his lips passionately. Aryan, fully aware of his surroundings, appeared stunned as she continued to kiss him passionately, their breath becoming heavier with each passing moment. After a while, as she dismounted Aryan, a silence fell upon them both. Lost in thought, he realized she had misunderstood his emotions. To clarify, he spoke softly, "All I can offer you is my solitude and silence, for that is what I have within me."

Listening to this, her smile grew wider as she said, "I can now feel your insatiable longing for love, which makes it impossible for me to stay away from you any longer."

Filled with annoyance, he tightened his grip around her neck, his words laced with bitterness. "You're fixated on my emotions, but you know damn well I have nothing to give you. If you continue to insist, then I will no longer consider you, my well-wisher."

With a smile on her face, she replied, "Your presence is what makes me feel complete. Your touch drives me to madness, leaving me consumed with both envy and the inability to express my love for you. From now on, I will completely reshape everything according to my desires, and you must accept it willingly or face my coercion."

As he listened to her words, he felt a heavy silence settle between them, realizing that she was seeking his validation of her emotions, an impossible task for him to fulfill. Without uttering a word, he silently retreated from the scene.

Reaching his house, he spends the whole day pondering why he didn't intervene when he could halt everything. Pondering it for a while, he documented all his sentiments, each occurrence, and the unforeseen turn of events that transpired in his life within the pages of his diary. After mentioning it all, he carefully placed his diary in a secure spot, his voice trembling as he said, "I want you to decide our fate. Will we remain intertwined as one soul, or will my sudden sins in your absence be the reason for your departure? I am unable to provide any proof or words to explain what happened to me when you left. So, I entrusted everything to you, knowing that whatever decision you make, we will both embrace it with a smile."

19

Chapter Ninteen

After a few days,

Ever since that day, Aryan has been trapped in his house, haunted by the events that transpired and unable to find restful sleep. Suddenly, as he lay on his bed one night, he felt a presence surrounding him, gently embracing him with a sense of comfort that he couldn't resist. This feeling of care and tenderness filled him with a soothing patience, lulling him into a peaceful sleep. While resting, Aryan abruptly woke up, his senses heightened by the strange feeling in the air.

Divya, despite appearing cold, continued to look after him without rest, her eyes now appearing dull and unfocused. Without a second thought, he held her tightly, his arms creating a cocoon of warmth around her, ensuring she felt safe and secure as she drifted off to sleep next to him. Aryan's gaze falls upon Divya, who is now peacefully asleep, a stark contrast to the earlier scene where she covered herself in tears, her eyes conveying an unspoken apology and a hint of fear in facing him.

After some time, she slowly awakens, greeted by Aryan's calm voice wishing her good morning, his words dripping with affection. Saying this, he carefully picked up the breakfast he had already prepared. After making her eat it all, he then leaves her to rest for a while longer. While in the living area where he was working, he couldn't help but think about her smile, which had vanished since that day.

Unable to contain herself any longer, she came rushing back to heal him upon learning of his pain. She simply couldn't bear to let him go. In the midst of it all, she loses sight of herself and remains more concerned with his happiness than her own well-being, constantly on edge, dreading his potential rudeness and cruelty, which fills him with overwhelming guilt, denying him any sense of peace. Feeling tense and uneasy, he quickly left the place, leaving her alone in her peaceful slumber.

Later at night,

As she slowly woke up from her sleep, she glanced around and realized she was alone in the room. With a sense of urgency, she got out of bed and attempted to turn on the lights, but to her dismay, nothing happened. With the flash of her phone illuminating the way, she cautiously descended the stairs into an eerie silence. Suddenly, she heard a faint voice coming from the last room, a room that was always kept locked. With courage, she entered the room and the door closed on its own. Suddenly, a flash of light illuminated the dark room where she stood in the center of a circle.

While looking at it, someone suddenly attempted to snatch the flash from her hand. Startled, she turned to the side and found herself face-to-face with Aryan. He gently took the flash from her, standing silently before her. As she looked at his carefully arranged setup, everything was just as she liked it. Slowly, he played a soft tune, taking her hands and gently placing them near his neck. Then, he wrapped his arms around her waist, drawing her closer. He slowly slid his hand from her lower back to gently lift her up, their bodies swaying in perfect rhythm to the music. Ignoring his gaze, she continued with her actions, prompting him to inquire, "Are you trying to evade my realm?"

While she listened to him, she couldn't help but notice the sadness in his eyes, a silent confession of the guilt he bore for hurting her. As she read this, tears welled up in her eyes, and she whispered, "I want to apologize..."

Until she could complete her words, he continued, "I want to apologize for my actions, for my harsh words, and especially for how I treated you. I can't bear the weight of hurting you, and it drains all the patience out of me, even when we're close. It now won't let me hold you with ease like I used to; I miss the way your hand fit perfectly in mine."

Slowly kissing her hand, he finally mustered the courage to ask, "Will you forgive me? Besides your forgiveness, I desire nothing else from you. All I ask is for your apology, to restore me to the man I once was. My well-wisher, will you find it in your heart to forgive me?"

With tears streaming down her face, she looked at him and said, "Why are you holding me back when I want to apologize? Every single one of those words belonged to me, and the burden of guilt weighed heavily on my conscience. You took everything from me, and now you won't even let me express myself. Can't you give me a chance to ask for your forgiveness?"

"I could never imagine," he replied, "that my well-wisher would ask for an apology. Instead of you, I want to ask for your forgiveness, the one who always blessed me with her selfless care. By hurting intentionally this time, I've lost sight of the real you. Now, all I desire is to have my beloved well-wisher back, the one who constantly showers me with smiles and care."

She responded, "You asked me to be full of myself, but there's nothing left for me to give, as you've already taken everything from me. At long last, my heart, which used to be caring, is now filled with nothing but pain."

Instantly, he uttered the words, "Treat me the way you want," leaving her heart racing with anticipation.

While she remained quiet, he went on, "I need you to acknowledge the darkness within me and grant yourself the freedom to treat me as you've always longed to."

While listening to this, she leaned in and gently kissed both of his eyes, a tender gesture of forgiveness for all he had done to her. He felt a wave of relief wash over him, and he gently kissed her forehead, whispering, "I can't express how I felt when I saw tears in your eyes. I felt completely helpless at that time, unable to figure out how to make them stop it. Your smile is my everything; losing it means losing everything I had."

As they hold each other tightly, she assures him, "I will never leave you, not today or even in your dreams," and they apologize to each other, making this night a good one for both.

20

Chapter Twenty

On the next day,

When Divya woke up from her sleep, she anxiously searched for Aryan, but he was nowhere to be found. Moving down, she discovers a breakfast spread on the table, complete with a note indicating that he's running late for college.

While reading his note, she navigated through the cluttered table, where his projects were haphazardly arranged. Observing this, she carefully organizes everything systematically, and, in the process, she stumbles upon his diary. Resting on top of it is a note that simply says, "For my well-wisher."

Taking the note, she reads, her eyes scanning the words carefully. Suddenly, she stops and her gaze drifts towards her room. Retrieving the note that Aryan had first handed to her, she unfolds it and reads it again. In her pursuit of the story, she finally unraveled the truth - it was not a declaration of his feelings, but a composition of vivid portrayal of the joy and beauty that Divya's presence could bring to his life.

As she read the words, a look of shock crossed her face. As he never said that he loved her and she misunderstood him, still he humbly accepted his mistake and acknowledged her feelings, which she had coerced him into admitting. She couldn't help but feel guilty as she thought about what she had done to him.

Feeling tense, she anxiously reached for his diary, hoping to find any mention of this incident and uncover his true feelings. As she read further, she discovered that there was no mention of the incident, but he vividly described how her presence had transformed his life. In a tense state, she ripped her page out of his diary, ensuring her sister would never find it. In doing so, she also erased her presence from his life, a reality she had forced him to accept. Filled with restlessness, she couldn't bear to stay in the house any longer and abruptly departed.

It had been a couple of days since she left, and even though she was in college, she kept herself occupied with work, completely ignoring Aryan. He tried often to reach out to her, but she always greeted him with the same distant demeanor, as if he were a stranger. Trapped in a life of solitude, he would always rush out of college, paying no attention to the captivating tune that played in the background. However, one day, he couldn't resist the urge to stop and listen, feeling as though the melody was meant only for him.

As he reached the dimly lit place, he noticed a girl attempting to dance to the beat of the music but continuously stumbling. Thinking it was Divya, he felt a surge of familiarity as the tune played, leading him to slowly step closer and gently take her hand from behind. He started practicing the same steps, effortlessly guiding her through each movement, until they could perform them with ease. Finally, he added his own flair to the steps, elevating the routine, and the tune came to a beautiful end. Without glancing at her face, he asked, "Do you still hold affection for me?"

Suddenly, applause erupted from behind him, as he found himself encircled by a crowd of college students who had gathered for the dance audition. Without waiting for a response, he quickly turned and left, leaving his words hanging in the air. For the past couple of days, he noticed how she acted strangely, clearly tense about something that happened in the past. Remembering this, he starts walking towards her, thinking of asking what it is that troubles her so deeply, that she can't even confide in him?

As he reached the spot where she was rehearsing, he noticed she was alone. Slowly, he approached her, his hand gently gliding over her waist from behind. "Just don't say a word," he whispered, "I won't ask for anything else. Right now, all I want is to dance with you, to find a moment of calm. I've been feeling so lonely for such a long time, and I'm filled with tension. Can you please share this moment with me?"

Silently, he began to sway with her to the music, completely engrossed in her presence, yet unable to decipher her thoughts. When the tune finally ends, he gently presses his lips against her neck, feeling a strange sensation. In response, he turns to her to face him. Instead of Divya, he now saw a completely different girl, and his expression instantly shifted to one of shock. Realizing his mistake, he wasted no time in apologizing to her, expressing his sincere regret. "I am really sorry, I thought you were someone else."

As he was leaving, she spoke up, saying, "I might not be the right person, but I can sense the genuineness of your emotions." However, he paid no attention to her words and departed.

21
Chapter Twenty One

After few days,

While attending his lecture, Aryan's attention was caught by the arrival of a new student. The professor introduced her to the class and assigned her the task of covering the semester. After finding the right person, he appoints Aryan to assist her in finishing her previous syllabus. As he listened, he glanced at her side, and in that moment of eye contact, memories of their last meeting flooded back. He remembered how he had mistaken her for Divya.

Slowly, she joins him on the same bench, taking the opposite corner. Upon seeing her again, he noticed a flush spreading across her cheeks, prompting him to quickly leave the place. As she watched him walk away without offering any assistance, she finally decided to leave. But before she departed, she noticed his forgotten notebook lying on the desk. Curiosity got the better of her, and she opened it to find a heartfelt apology on the very first page.

"I'm sorry for what happened before. This note will assist you in completing your previous syllabus."

During his lecture, Aryan quietly shares his notes with her, without even exchanging a glance or a word. After completing her lecture one day, she was approached by a few girls from her class who asked her to join them for some fun. She agreed and they led her to the secluded side of the college where few people ventured. After navigating through the messy path, they finally arrived at the hidden party spot, which had been kept a secret on the college grounds for the past few months.

Upon arrival, the air was filled with the lively beats of music, the energetic movements of dancing, and the mingling scents of drugs and alcohol. Despite feeling unsafe, she mustered the courage to step into the unfamiliar place where college students warmly greeted everyone. Upon seeing the new girl, they made an effort to welcome her, but things took a turn when a group of girls started drinking and pressured her into joining them, hoping to liven up the party and help her forget her tense mood.

After a while, as she became intoxicated, she clumsily tried to adapt to her surroundings. A guy made a move on her, touching her inappropriately, so she asked her friends to leave the place where everyone seemed to be under the influence of drugs. Just as she walks alone to leave, she finds herself cornered by a few guys who persistently ask her to stay and enjoy the party. The music abruptly stopped, catching everyone's attention. DJ and other crew members rushed to set it back up but could not do so. It turned out that Aryan had intentionally cut off the music, and in an instant, he illuminated the room with a flick of the switch. Walking inside, he notices the partygoers, heavily intoxicated and completely unaware.

Finally, he reaches her and without a word, he holds her hand, signaling the other girls to leave before quietly leaving the room with her. He then pauses and locks the room from the outside, ensuring no one can escape. Taking the girls to the backside garden, he gave them medication to regain consciousness.

He noticed that Divya's guards and staff were all headed in the same direction, evacuating everyone and apprehending those involved with the help of security and police. He appeared shocked when he noticed Divya standing in front of him, who had tracked him down. Instead of looking at him, she glanced at all the girls he was administering medication to. She halted her men from handing the girls over to the police, and Aryan attempted to express his gratitude, but she departed.

22

Chapter Twenty Two

On the next day,

While leaving his lecture, Aryan suddenly pauses upon seeing the audition list on the soft board. He ripped it immediately and as he was leaving, he noticed Divya standing with the college staff, who then put up another list. As he looked at it, he suggested, "It would be best to ask the participants first if they will participate in the dance competition or not."

Just as he was about to leave, Divya interjected, "I have seen your impressive dance skills, so I have added your name to the list. Furthermore, if you are having trouble finding the perfect dance partner, I have already arranged a partner for you."

She points to the new girl, "You dance so well with her," she remarks, observing the beautiful connection they share, a captivating sight on the stage.

Observing her words, he seemed taken aback, understanding precisely why she was upset with him. Soon, he walked closer to her, his voice filled with desperation as he pleaded, "Please don't do this to me. It's not fair. You know very well that my feet refuse to move with anyone else but you."

Divya replied, her voice filled with anger and determination, "I have witnessed it all with my own eyes, and now you will pay for everything. I want you to feel the pain that I endure every day, seeing her in your arms, where only my right should be."

Aryan's voice finally broke the silence as he stated, "I'm sorry, but I won't be able to join in. I have other tasks to attend to."

She yelled, her voice dripping with sarcasm, "Now you will teach me ethics? You are no longer employed, and there is no longer a need for you to work in the library or on any college campus. I am freeing you from ethical restraints so you can focus solely on practicing and performing your new composed tune at the college event, which will surely captivate the crowd. The college's reputation will be restored to its former glory, which you single-handedly destroyed. I intentionally assigned you the task of recovering everything I lost in the past few days."

Aryan's silence spoke volumes as he listened to everything. Now, he avoids eye contact and stays quiet, overwhelmed with embarrassment. Eventually, he quietly exits the scene.

After 1 week,

Aryan sat silently in the lecture room, observing the professor's words with rapt attention. As the room emptied, he mustered the courage to tap the unknown girl's shoulder and asked, "Do you genuinely believe that I have the potential to be a skilled dancer or a good partner?"

Aryan, finally speaking to her for the first time, made her turn to his side. She replied, "You were always the best at everything from the beginning, but now you seem to ignore everything after that event."

He swiftly stood up from his seat and took a few steps closer to her, his voice laced with fury. "Ever since you came into my life, everything has been a disaster. You're nothing but a troublemaker. So, it would be best if you keep your distance from me after this.

As he was departing, she declared, "My name is Jahnavi Shukla, and while you may view me as a curse, I see you as a cherished wish I want to protect forever."

Moving closer, she continued, "Since the day you entered my life, everything has become interesting. People are now paying more attention to me, all because my name and presence are associated with you. Your deeds bring me nothing but grace and wisdom. So, tell me, should I call you my well-wisher after this?"

She observed him listening intently, but he seemed silent and eager to depart. Holding his hand, she said, "Like a coin, I have two sides. One may hurt you, but the other could heal you. If my presence has caused you pain, let my other side heal you with compassion and care. Consider experiencing the other side as well."

As he listened, irritation etched across his face, he suddenly lunged forward, wrapping his hand around her throat. "Miss Trouble," he hissed, "you've caused enough harm. I never want to see you again."

With a slow smile, she spoke, "I never meddle in your life; it's you who entered mine, and now you blame me for everything."

As he listens in silence, he slowly let go of her throat and silently departs.

23
Chapter Twenty Three

The other day,

After attending his lecture, Aryan noticed Divya, along with some men and staff members, waiting for him as he left the class. He was injected with medication until he became unconscious, unable to comprehend anything. Upon waking up, Aryan found himself chained and trapped in a dark room. He had been waiting all day in the dark when he finally saw Divya approaching him, and before he could utter a word, she kissed him passionately.

Progressing further, she passionately kisses him all over his body while he remains silent and allows her to take charge. When she remains unsettled for a while, he tightly embraces her with his chained hand, causing her to glance in his direction.

She expressed, "During my lonely nights, I longed for you... I need you now, my well-wisher, I can't bear to be apart from you any longer."

Hearing her words, he scooped her up in his arms. He leaves the dark room and walks to his class, where he sits on the back bench. There were so many questions left unanswered, but they sat in silence, their eyes locked on each other. He then gently guided her hand to rest on his chest, right above his beating heart, and inquired, "Don't you want to know what emotions are coursing through me at this moment?"

She said, "I already have stolen much of your precious moment on which only her right was there, but I took it all for me."

He replied, "but you always wanted to know how I feel, exclusively for you, even if it's just once."

With a pained expression, she implored him, "I don't want to go back to the moments where I hurt you. And if you force me to remember the emptiness of losing you, then you won't have the opportunity to see me ever again."

He asked, "What will happen to us when she returns to me? Are you scared for that day?"

As she listened to the exact point, which was hurting her the most, her eyes filled with tears. Sitting in front, her state began to plummet as she contemplated the impending day when he would leave her life. In response, she tightened her grip on his body, desperate to keep him close. Noticing her insecurity, he leaned in and planted soft kisses on her cheeks and nose, reassuring her with each gentle touch.

"I will never let you go," he whispered, his voice filled with conviction. "You're a permanent part of my life and my dreams. No matter the harm you caused or the individuals who will enter my life, I am unaware of the future's course for us. I have experienced both my happiest and most challenging moments with you, but despite it all, I still desire you in my life."

Aryan's presence brought her a sense of calm, as he promised to stay by her side until she had released all her anxieties about losing him. With sincerity in his voice, he declared his love for her, urging her to consider the consequences of her actions, for they would affect them both.

She said in a hushed voice, "I have already caused enough harm, and if I stay any longer, more mistakes will occur. Please, don't try to stop me any further."

Aryan asked, his voice filled with confusion, "If you really wanted to go, why are you still in my arms? Why won't you let me be alone when I am lost? Tell me, what's preventing you from walking away from me?"

"I really don't know how you could still treat me with care," she asked, her voice filled with wonder. "Even after knowing that I see no limits, doing anything whether I do my best or do my worst. But still, you wished to have my presence. Why?"

He replied, "faith... it was the unwavering faith someone had in me when I was at my lowest, and now when I look at you, I see a reflection of myself in need of my assistance. Moreover, despite knowing that I can never be yours because of my past, you still chose to embrace my dark side. So, how can I possibly let you go without a fight?"

He gazes into her eyes and echoes her words, "There is no substitute for you in my life. I either have you as you are, or I remain lonely without you. No one else can take your place or your memories. I won't allow this to happen, no one can take it away from me, not even you. I possess it and will forever protect you in my heart."

Upon hearing his confession in real, which had previously confused her, she then sought reassurance, saying, "Promise me that you will always be this way for me, because I don't want anything else from you after this."

Upon her request, he wasted no time in kissing her forehead and making a lifelong commitment. Then she appeared calm, and the terrible night transformed into a peaceful dawn, as they drifted off to sleep while holding each other.

24

Chapter Twenty Four

Later in the morning,

As Aryan slept, he could feel her gentle touch, playfully teasing him. Overwhelmed by dizziness, he pulled her closer, embracing her tightly as he planted soft kisses on her neck and cheeks. Feeling a sense of intimacy, she moves closer and begins to passionately kiss him, exploring with her tongue and occasionally biting down, gradually unleashing her wild side. Aryan then tried to calm her overwhelming emotions that were growing stronger. He gently kissed her forehead and whispered, "I am here, my..." She finished his sentence, saying, "Miss Trouble..."

As soon as he heard her name, he jolted awake from his slumber. From the classroom window, he caught a glimpse of Divya making her way to class. Without hesitation, he reached out and grabbed Jahnavi's hand, quickly ducking behind the wall, anticipating Divya's passing. Divya entered the class, but upon finding it empty, she left.

After she leaves, Aryan turns to Miss Trouble, noticing the mark of her lipstick on his neck and chest. He abruptly pulled her closer, gripping her neck, and asked, "Is this your lipstick stain?"

Her voice trembled as she replied, "Yes!"

His voice filled with anger, he confronted her, saying, "Miss trouble, I want you to make these marks disappear."

Upon hearing this, she immediately clutched his shirt tightly, pulling him closer as she passionately kissed him, leaving her marks all over his body while sensually pleasuring him, causing the spot to fade away. She glares at him angrily as he tightly grips her hair, causing her to wince in pain, which only seems to fuel his excitement.

In this situation where he always pleaded for her to keep her distance, she noticed his desperation as she carefully removed the stain, trying to please him. Lost in the process, she finally found her way and completed it. In a tender moment, she pressed her lips against his neck, her kiss filled with passion, as she pleaded, "Please stay with me in this moment."

In the midst of his angry outburst, he forcefully tugged at her hair, causing her to flinch, while his eyes bore into her with fury, cautioning her, "Never try to play games with me ever again."

Later at night,

When Aryan arrived home, he discovered the door was unlocked. Upon entering the house, the sound of a tune emanating from the last room greeted him. Upon arrival, he noticed Divya playing the piano and reading the new composition that he had exclusively sent to their studio partner. He moves closer to her, observing as she effortlessly plays the tune. "You remind me of someone," he said, "who effortlessly plays the tune on my composition, filling the room with beautiful melodies."

With a smile on her face, she turned to leave when he suddenly asked, "How did you unlock this house?"

She replied without hesitation, "I can manage anything to come close to you." The weight of her words hung in the air as he asked, shocked, "Did you also buy this house like you took over Anjali's assets?"

Turning back, she walks closer to him, her voice filled with hesitation as she asks, "If I reveal the truth, will it shatter your heart. Are you still willing to listen?"

Aryan stood motionless, his curiosity still burning within him. Divya finally answered, "I nearly took everything from her, but then

I stumbled upon this house. Unfortunately, it can't be in my name because she purchased it from yours, using her own hard-earned money. When I came to know about this, my heart overflowed with blessings for her. She not only bought this house, but also invested in her happiness. I really can't fathom the depth of her need for you, but her love for you knows no bounds. We are insignificant compared to the love she has for you."

Upon hearing this, he immediately embraced her tightly, expressing his gratitude for keeping Anjali's other gift safe. Overwhelmed by warm emotions, she couldn't resist and whispered, "I promise to safeguard your precious gifts, untouchable by anyone, even myself."

25
Chapter Twenty Five

One day, as Aryan was leaving college, Jahnavi couldn't help but glance at Divya, who had her eyes fixed on him until he disappeared through the college gate. Standing close to her, she whispered, "Whenever I see him in pain, my heart can't help but be drawn to him."

Divya turned to her side, her voice filled with suspicion, and said, "I know exactly what you're up to and I'm aware of your intentions. But I don't think you will achieve what you're aiming for."

She was leaving, but Jahnavi asked, "You've tried everything, but none of it works, right?"

Upon hearing this, Divya responded, "Let's head to my office and discuss some business, shall we?"

Sitting in the office where Divya starts the meeting by introducing herself, "So, I'm Divya Shukla, the CEO of this College. You're just a student at this college, Jahnavi Shukla, who's now into Aryan Mishra. Let me show it to you," she said, pressing play on the recording. Jahnavi's passionate kisses with Aryan echoed through the room. Jahnavi questioned her, "If you're aware of everything, why do you still maintain your silence?"

Divya then replied, "even in his sleep, he dreams of someone precious, allowing you to come close as he thinks of her. I remain silent, placing my trust in him as he continues to fight for her return. I made a promise to stand behind him, offering my unwavering support, and I am determined to shield him from anything that might cause him pain. Take note of this and avoid bothering him from now on."

While leaving in silence, she finally mustered the courage to ask her, "If you don't fight for yourself, how could he ever be yours?"

Divya appeared composed at first, but as she watched the recording of Jahnavi taking care of him, her anger rose. Eventually, she couldn't contain it any longer and urgently called someone to handle everything immediately. With a composed demeanor, she patiently waits for the desired outcome to manifest.

After a while, she went to meet up with the new interns who were visiting the college. As she greeted them, they embarked on a tour of the college seminar and cultural events, where they witnessed various programs and practices in action. Moving further, she suddenly came to a halt and glanced at the bustling photo gallery capturing different angles of the college, where one image caught her attention. Seeing the urgent need for the new documents, she quickly called her men to bring them to her in the library. However, Aryan, who happened to be passing through, was stopped by her men.

He turned to her, where she stood holding a fresh document that she promptly handed to him. Without exchanging a word, he made a move to tear the document, but she abruptly intervened, preventing him from doing so. She said, "I am appointing you as the ambassador of our college. Your song and presence will bring attention to this institution, making you the face of our college. To make this happen, you have to sign the contract and you will be paid 1 lakh rupees for each month."

When he saw the contract appointing him as the official model of Divya enterprise, he urgently tried to stop her. Suddenly, one of the interns emerges, holding a camera and eagerly displaying pictures of Aryan, highlighting his irresistible charm. He slowly turns to the person and looks shocked, then asks Divya, "What's she doing here?"

Divya said, "We've got some new interns joining our college soon. I'm selecting a few of them who are talented in various arts and subjects. They'll also help us with our events."

He stayed quiet while Divya waited for him to sign the contract. Suddenly, that person rushed and got Aryan's thumbprint on the contract, then gave it to Divya. Divya observed his annoyed expression, yet he remained silent in the presence of that person. Turning to Akanchha Mishra, she said, "I believe we have some unfinished business. Please accompany me so we can take care of all the procedures."

Hearing this, he tightly grasped his sister's hand, bringing her to a halt, and sternly told Divya, "She won't be signing any documents until I've seen them first." Saying that, he walks away accompanied by his sister.

In the canteen, they sit quietly as they continue to wait for the document. Divya eventually arrived with her team and college staff, bringing the necessary documents. Once he finished reading it, he asked the men to add a new line stating that she will be allowed to continue her internship only if she scores 90% in her intermediate. Until then, she will only serve as his official photographer, and any damage will be attributed to him, not his sister.

The lines were added, and then he signed the contract, followed by his sister. After that, they left silently, their footsteps barely making a sound, as Divya appeared convinced that he would now attend college every day. Furthermore, she will have full control over him, as he willingly surrendered his rights to her, which ultimately leads to her departure.

26

Chapter Twenty Six

Now, Aryan comes to college every day. He diligently completes his work and routine. After that, he spends his time looking after his sister's work and projects, preparing for the college event. One day, while Akanchha was sitting in silence, Jahnavi quietly joined her, and they sat side by side without uttering a word for several days. During times of heavy workload, Jahnavi would quietly lend a hand with event work, but one day as she was leaving, Aryan intercepted her.

He said, "I see you getting along with my sister now a days which I don't like; the tension in his voice was palpable.

Her voice trembled slightly as she replied, "She doesn't get hurt even when I meet her every day, so I must not pose a threat to anyone. Only you despise my company, but I always admire you whenever our paths cross." Disregarding what she said, he departs and gives her a new note to finish her semester.

While working one day, Akanchha left her things and Divya's men gave them to Divya. Observing her work, she appears in awe of event preparation. While inspecting, she comes across Anjali's photo hidden among her brother's possessions and promptly shuts her things.

Akanchha, who was in a rush to find her things at college, finally spotted Divya returning them to her. She thanks her, but Divya indirectly gives her a task: "You can thank me once you assist me in finishing the unfinished task that you have kept safe in your belongings." Akanchha is left to contemplate as she returns to her work. When she remains quiet, Jahnavi inquires, "Are you troubled by something? Why do you seem lost? Let me know if there's anything I can do to assist you."

Jahnavi remains silent after hearing Akanchha's words and decides to leave. Akanchha stated firmly, "My sole purpose for coming to this college was to take care of my brother."

Jahnavi stops and says, "because he is still lonely, his pain a constant companion that he keeps hidden from the world."

As she listened to the same fact about his brother, she appeared astonished, and their relationship seemed to improve as they bonded over their shared issue. Eventually, she repeated the exact words that Divya had asked her, saying, "You can show your gratitude by helping me complete the unfinished task that you've been keeping safe in your belongings."

As she handed her belongings to Jahnavi, she confessed, "I tried my best, but I couldn't ease my brother's loneliness." Her words hung in the air, heavy with disappointment. She says this and then leaves, leaving Jahnavi alone with Aryan's things for the whole day.

Divya, who was walking by, suddenly stopped when Jahnavi handed her the exact item, she had asked Akanchha to find. Jahnavi said, "You have one opportunity to either restore your college's reputation or support him, but there's a chance you might lose him forever."

Divya took the stuff from her hand, her expression turning silent and contemplative. She didn't open it until Akanchha entered the meeting room. Excitedly, she tells her, "We have found a work that will bring wonders to our college event. Furthermore, if you lend your assistance, I can assure you that your career will flourish under my company's banner, and you will also receive a full scholarship for your advanced studies. So, will you help me?"

While hearing her offer, she questioned, "Is the risk so great that you require my involvement?"

Divya responded, "If it's not you, then nobody else could do it."

"Count me in," Akanchha said without hesitation.

While Akanchha and Jahnavi worked together, a group of college students, looking for new interns, arrived. He appeared thrilled to see her with his previous crush, as if he had acquired two beauties at once. Despite his attempts at flirting, they pay him no attention. While walking one day, Stud found themselves surrounded by college girls in the main ground, each holding a Rakhi. In that group, he saw both his girlfriend and his crush, making his heart race.

Seeing this, he yelled, "What on earth are you doing?"

They continued on towards their group, the silence hanging heavy in the air as they approached to celebrate Raksha-Bandhan. As they stood in opposition, Aryan appeared, offering each girl a stud to secure the knot. Only a few of the main studs were left, so he chose their girlfriends and crushes to tie rakhi, against his will.

Divya's men rushed towards the sudden gathering in the main ground, attempting to intervene, but the dense crowd blocked their way. Upon seeing this, Divya immediately instructed his men to disperse the crowd by any means necessary. As they made way towards the center, she noticed all the stud hands filled with rakhis. "What's happening?" she asked, curious.

Akanchha and Jahnavi, the only ones left to tie the rakhi, did so instantly, resulting in smiles on their faces while everyone else was scared by their actions today. Witnessing this, Divya refrained from asking any more questions and instructed everyone to depart. Aryan, who is sitting calmly in the library, notices that Divya is waiting for an explanation for his intentional actions today. Ignoring her anger, he departs silently with a smile.

27

Chapter Twenty Seven

The next day,

The entire college appeared shocked as they gazed at the poster for the yesterday's event. They all start removing it. Out of nowhere, a student played a news clip about a social event held at National IT college where every picture was chosen as the best event picture ever taken. Divya, Akanchha, and Jahnavi were on the front, with everyone else being silent, waiting for Aryan.

Upon entering the college, he was intercepted by Divya's men, with Divya eagerly awaiting his explanation. Noticing the silence, he inquired, "Are you not fond of the gift that highlights your college?"

As he was about to leave, Divya asked someone, "Whose idea was this?"

A voice from the crowd calls out the name Aryan. He turns with a smile when he realizes it's his sister. Upon witnessing this, he proceeded to say, "If any mishap occurs, I should be held responsible for all charges." Since he shows no concern, she proceeds to give him the one-month suspension notice.

Looking at the suspension letter, a smile spreads across his face as he confidently declares, "We are leaving now."

Divya firmly holds Akanchha's hand and reassures him, "She won't leave. I have written consent from her parents for her internship." She shows him the notice, bearing her parents' signature.

Aryan glanced at his sister, who seemed unwilling to go and sought refuge behind Divya. Feeling despondent, he uttered a single phrase to Divya, "I'm walking away for now, but if anything goes awry, I'll set fire to your cherished college and all its reputation - a place you hold dear. This time, no one will be able to intervene, not even you."

Saying this, he was making his way to the library, when suddenly her men intercepted him and she delivered the news, "You've already been terminated from your librarian position, so there's no need for you to handle anything else." Upon hearing her words, he stops in his tracks and hands her the diary. "If not me, then please make sure this diary is returned to where it belongs," and left.

28
Chapter Twenty Eight

Akanchha has been avoiding everyone for a few days now. Divya tried to calm her down, but Akanchha got aggressive, saying, "You tricked me into helping you with my brother's issues, and it's ruining his career. But you totally tricked me when you suspended him because he never listens to anyone. He faced suspension for his acts of helping others, and I was also entangled in the situation, resulting in his unforgiving attitude towards me. Your selfishness destroyed a beautiful sibling relationship; may you experience the pain of being separated from your loved one's due to someone else's mistake."

Jahnavi witnessed everything as Akanchha left while saying this. Jahnavi, who had difficulty getting along with Divya, now feels sorry for her as she continues to try to help Aryan, which no one can comprehend. Just as Divya was about to leave, Jahnavi's words rang out, "I've said it before and I'll say it again, this task will only bring destruction to every relationship involved, including yours and his sister's. Everything will crumble in the end. There's still time to reverse it and bring things back to how they were." Divya departs silently, without uttering a word.

Now, both Divya and Akanchha have cut ties with Aryan, and as a result, their once peaceful state of mind is slowly fading away. One day, as Divya left college, Jahnavi stumbled upon Aryan's diary. Reluctantly, she skimmed through it and caught a glimpse of Divya's deepest emotions. After reading it, she closed the diary at once and now feels a surge of sympathy for Divya. She realizes that Divya only suggested the plan and now everyone has turned against her. Despite all this, she still wants what's best for Aryan. However, her actions have now framed her as the culprit in the eyes of Aryan and his sister, and she knows she needs to fix this perception.

Aryan, who was feeling lonely, unexpectedly caught sight of Jahnavi. "Don't you want to know how everything is going?" she inquired.

Aryan stops in his tracks as she confesses that his sister feels remorse but lacks the bravery to confront him. However, he remained unresponsive and prepared to depart. Before he left, she felt compelled to assist someone else and returned his diary, remarking, "I cannot say whether this is correct or incorrect, but I took a risk in delivering this diary to you. Perhaps it will aid in altering your perspective of us."

Divya went back to the library after a few days, hoping to reconnect with her emotions, but to her dismay, her diary was nowhere to be found. As she saw Jahnavi sneaking into the library, a look of concern crossed her face, realizing that no one besides Aryan knew about the diary. Aware of this, she waits for her.

Jahnavi, upon going to the library this time, she sees Divya waiting for her. As soon as she walked in, she played the recording. After examining it, she declared, "I don't want to hear anything. I just want my diary back, or else you'll pay for this." From behind her, a voice said, "It has already been returned to its rightful owner."

She turned to the side and declared, "No one can take away my feelings, not even Aryan, who is the only one entitled to them."

Finally, Akanchha asked, "If you say you care about him, why do you always intentionally hurt him?"

Divya falls silent upon hearing this, unable to justify it to herself. Seeing this, Jahnavi stops Akanchha from advancing, and she immediately leaves. Divya, who lost her emotions because of Jahnavi, remained silent as Akanchha took the blame and left quietly. When Jahnavi was leaving, she noticed Akanchha standing alone and looking at the big tree. Jahnavi approached her and asked, "Why did you save me?"

"Did you meet my brother?" she asked.

Jahnavi mentioned that she tried to resolve everything, but he refuses to listen to anyone.

Akanchha replied, "he will not listen to anyone other than his mysterious friend who abandoned him and this college that he desperately tried to keep hidden from us. But now, when he's injured, there's no one to care for him."

Jahnavi noticed the tension in both Akanchha and Divya after that day. She was contemplating while looking at Aryan's belongings, and in that moment, she impulsively snapped a photo of him. Later, she decided to post it on the college social media before leaving.

29

Chapter Twenty Nine

The other day,

Sitting in her cabin, Divya observed a sudden surge in company shares and received enticing offers, tempting her to embark on a new venture in modeling and fashion designing. While she was looking at it, she heard the head dean approaching, asking if she had seen the cover page of the fashion magazine. They were in search of an Aryan face for their new campaign.

"I don't care at all, so please just go away," she said with a dismissive tone.

As he listened, a look of shock crossed his face when he realized her complete lack of interest. Before leaving, he suggested, "You once mentioned wanting to restore your college's prestige. Maybe bringing back Aryan is the key to achieving that. From the past few events, it has become evident that everyone adores his music, compositions, looks, and style. In fact, some even wish to sign a contract with him. However, we both know he will never accept any of it because he doesn't want to betray this college, not today or in the future. It's wise to think twice before making any decision, to ensure you make the best choice.

Just as he was about to leave, Divya questioned, "What makes you trust him so deeply and believe that he will come back to this college?"

Upon hearing this, he abruptly stops in his tracks and turns towards her, a smile spreading across his face. He then confidently declares, "When it comes to him, I trust him even more than my own son. I have no doubt that he will return. This college holds all the memories of his best and worst moments, which still linger here."

With those words lingering in the air, he walks away, leaving her to ponder. Thinking about this, she diligently searched for the originator's post on the company site. When she realizes that it's Jahnavi again, her temper flares up, but instead of erupting in anger, she becomes eerily quiet. Thinking about something important, she quickly organized an impromptu meeting at the college, bringing together new interns, staff members from the company, and college personnel.

She immediately uploaded an official face for her new campaign on the college portal and now sits in silence, as it gradually starts capturing everyone's attention. Within an hour, numerous likes and comments poured in, urging her to share more of her new looks and style. Finally, they also request the release of her unfinished composition.

Seeing this, Dean stood and said, "The face before us is not ordinary, but the embodiment of this college's spirit, capable of bringing wonders to our institution. If we plan accordingly and start a new campaign, we can all earn significant profits while enhancing the college's reputation and prestige. So, I now leave this decision in your hands. What will you choose to do next?"

Soon, a group of students arrived, causing a commotion in the college. Some demanded his banishment while others advocated for his release, leading to disturbances. Despite this, she continues the meeting where numerous staff and company partners express their doubts about his abilities, stating that he brings trouble and often makes mistakes in this institution. Moreover, he's already a suspended student, losing his chance to play with college prestige. Therefore, we won't invest in this campaign and will decline the offer.

Divya respectfully listened to everyone's negative votes for the campaign, understanding and accepting their decisions. "As everyone reached a consensus on the negative side, we will proceed with the meeting's decision. This means that we will no longer appoint him as the face of the college and his compositions will no longer be released under the college's name."

As everyone filed out of the meeting room, their satisfied murmurs filled the air, but Divya remained behind, captivated by the picture of Aryan.

30

Chapter Thirty

After few days,

Divya, with a lingering gaze at the campaign poster, suddenly received a call from an unknown private number. Answering the call, she rose from her seat and instructed the driver to proceed to the requested destination. As she arrived, her eyes met the gaze of the rival company staff eagerly waiting for her. She sits down and waits for the CEO. After a while, Jahnavi arrives and takes a prominent seat, presenting a new deal to her. Observing the identical proposal, she appears irritated and questions, "It's the same proposal that everyone turned down, and now you, as the CEO of my competitor, have shown up again. I'm not sure what your intentions are."

Jahanvi calmly states, "Not only your sister, but there are also others who possess the same power and royalty as she does and could be the CEO of their father's company. The proposal remains the same, but the company shares and even the site have changed from before."

Divya appears shocked as she discovers that it's a collaborative campaign, with Jahnavi's company taking charge and investing in everything. However, most of the shares will be in her name, prompting her to ask, "Why are you suggesting this to me?"

She answered, saying, "I'll contribute to this campaign, but the primary profit will be associated with my name. In this established firm, numerous brands, models, and designers work together to cater exclusively to you, resulting in substantial profits. But what's in it for you? You will regain possession of him, and this time, no contract or relationship can separate him from you. In our new firm, he won't be labeled as an expelled student and there will be no honor killings. Additionally, we have the option to publish his composition through our company. So, what is your preference?"

It's been a few days since they made their decision. All the new interns were requested to report to the new site. Upon arrival, Akanchha appeared shocked to find that it was a startup firm working on multiple things with various resources under one roof. However, she also seemed excited to be in a new location. Everything was going well for her until she discovered that all the work being done here was mostly her idea, which she proposed earlier.

Upon seeing this, she headed towards the CEO's cabin and discovered that all the work was related to a new campaign that had been rejected in college, yet this new firm was tirelessly working on it. While examining it, she eventually lit up the room and came across a portrait of Aryan that was an exact replica of the image she had taken and had in her belongings, but it was still in the process of being published. Witnessing this, she appeared startled and inquired about the owner of the firm, but no one ever entered this place.

Akanchha now arrives daily, completes her tasks, and finally departs with a fresh impression and Aryan-related materials for the campaign. Every day she leaves new things, only to be asked to work on the same thing the next day, which she had suggested. Now, upon seeing this, she really wants to meet the CEO.

Divya, who still longs for him, now seeks his hidden emotions, which inspires her to create a new melody. Divya stayed late at the site one day, taking care of the progress, when Akanchha arrived to deliver the new stuff. Sensing someone's presence, she immediately walked into the room where she found Divya gazing at Aryan's portrait. She walked slowly towards her, unable to take her eyes off the portrait, and asked Akanchha, "Didn't he look happy and calm in this portrait? I haven't seen him like this since his unique friend left him."

Hearing about his past made Akanchha emotional. Divya gently wiped away the tears from her eyes as she turned to her side, asking, "Do you remember when you asked me why I hurt him despite being his well-wisher? He denies living in the present because he is consumed by memories of the past. He once requested my care, and now I wish for him to regain life. Even if it means hurting him more, I'll bring back his smile like his 'unique friend' asked me to before leaving, and I'll keep that promise at any cost."

As she heard this, she immediately embraced her tightly, tears welling up in her eyes, holding her for a moment. She feels remorseful for saying hurtful things out of anger and has asked for forgiveness. She kissed her forehead slowly as she listened, trying to calm her.

Akanchha inquired, "How did you handle everything when both college and your firm turned down the proposal?"

Just as she was about to answer, Jahnavi shows up with a detailed presentation. As Akanchha carefully attended to every detail, she couldn't help but express her astonishment and inquire, "When did you start working on this project?"

Jahnavi acknowledged, Divya single-handedly managed everything, even when everyone abandoned her, with only a small contribution from Jahnavi to make the task happen.

Holding her hand with care, she thanked, "I am grateful to you that you always stay with me like this."

Jahnavi responded, "If you truly want to enhance Divya's task and your brother's career, there is one crucial step to make it our official project. We've been using your brother's belongings without his permission, and if he finds out, he might take legal action against us, which is the main concern."

Upon hearing this, Akanchha quickly responded, "If I sign this contract, our blood relation will ensure that he never goes against me. And since his sister is already involved in this project, he will ultimately sign the contract with you."

Jahnavi eagerly asked, "Do you think he will sign the contract with us?"

Without hesitation, Akanchha took the document and promptly signed the contract. Akanchha handed it to her and said, "You can officially invite him to your new firm where he will definitely come looking for his sister who just signed a new project without asking him. My task is to make him sign the contract, but I don't want to face his anger. So, who will handle this situation?

Akanchha left and put Aryan's new things on the desk. Divya's curiosity led her to examine the new items in front of her. Seeing her calm, Jahnavi then refrains from asking anything and silently starts to leave when Divya asks, "Why did you stop me from revealing that it was all your idea and not mine?"

As she listened, she turned to her side and caught a glimpse of her calm face, a gentle smile playing on her lips. Jahnavi replied, "To bring back your smile that vanished when he left, and to witness you slowly obtaining what I promised you. Not only will he commend you, but his sister will also express her gratitude once they find out what you've done for them."

Upon hearing this, Divya once again posed the same question, "What did you receive in exchange for doing all of this?"

Jahnavi smiled and proudly presented the contract, showcasing her signature. "I will have my profit," she said with a determined tone, emphasizing that only she could earn it. She left after saying, "I did all this for my profit, and I spent a lot."

In a hushed tone, Divya remarks, "She's a heartless woman who only values her wealth, not anyone's feelings."

Following this, Divya asked to send an official notice inviting Aryan to the firm. While leaving late one day, she noticed Aryan standing at the firm. Slowly, she walks towards him, her gaze tracing his figure from head to toe. As she approached, she noticed him disoriented, scanning the surroundings without making eye contact. "Girl, it's too late for you to be outside," he said to her before abruptly leaving.

31

Chapter Thirty One

He walked by himself to his house, climbed the stairs to his room, and just as he was about to lie down, he reached behind him and took hold of her hand, bringing her close to him before they both lay down. As she kissed him tenderly, her touch became a soothing balm for his weary body, and he held her tightly, revealing the loneliness he had endured in the silent darkness of the night.

Spending the entire night with him, he finally falls asleep while she gazes into his closed eyes, wondering if he's still angry with her despite holding her tightly. She caught sight of his diary and attempted to retrieve it, but then withdrew her hands and held him back before eventually falling asleep.

When Aryan woke up, he found himself alone, but felt peaceful this time. Observing that his diary was still there, he leaves. Akanchha and the rest of the staff were shocked to see Aryan walking into the firm with an invitation and heading towards the CEO's cabin. When he arrived, he found Divya sitting in the lamplight, feeling anxious in the darkness. The room was dark until he entered, flooding it with light and revealing his portrait and the extensive project that was underway.

She saw him standing in front of her, and even though she looked into his eyes, he took the contract without looking at her. Once he finished reading it, he reiterated his request to include the statement, "If anything goes wrong, all charges should be placed under my name."

Upon hearing this, she instructed to prepare the new contract. Aryan finally glanced at the previous contract, where his sister had signed. He signs the new contract after reclaiming his sister's freedom. "It was a pleasure doing business with you," he said, leaving with a heavy heart.

As soon as he arrived in the main area, everyone crowded around him, and he seemed irritated. Without consulting me, no one else may decide when and on what things my consent is needed. He tore the previous contract in front of them to make that clear. He threw the contract and left, saying, "Remember my words, I won't repeat them."

Other staff members, along with Akanchha, appear terrified of him as they thought, he refuses the project. Jahnavi arrives in the main area, presenting a new contract as proof of his official agreement with us. Everyone appeared excited upon seeing this, immediately returning to their work, except for Akanchha who paused while picking up the torn contract.

Jahnavi walked over to her after she had been sitting alone in silence, looking at the torn papers. Akanchha asked her, "The contract that was once useful in bringing back my brother is now just a torn piece of paper, reflecting how our relationship is slowly losing its bond."

Divya unexpectedly spoke up before anyone else, saying, "He originally came to reclaim your freedom, but when he discovered your involvement in this project, he willingly signed the contract for you."

Feeling a sense of calm, she confidently declared, "I am determined to meticulously compile a comprehensive project for my brother, showcasing that he placed his trust in the right person when he signed the contract."

Jahnavi interrupts Divya, emphasizing that their proposal is not a matter of family, and they should not jeopardize everything just to appease someone's emotions. "Akanchha Mishra," she replied, her voice filled with pride, "is no ordinary girl, especially considering she is blood-related to Aryan. As for Aryan, I see nothing, not even signing the contract, that I want to see after witnessing you hitting on him."

From her words, it was clear that she was angry. Before leaving, she said, "The person you cared about the most will eventually leave you, and then you'll come back to me to reclaim their rights."

With that said, she departs, leaving Divya to determine who she wants to grant project authority to.

32
Chapter Thirty Two

After 2 days,

Divya announced Jahnavi must approve all project decisions, and in her absence, either me or Akanchha should be approached. We need this project completed promptly since we have a team of new interns, staff, and recruits.

When everyone hears this, they all leave, leaving Akanchha feeling disappointed, but she manages to get back to work. Witnessing Divya's abrupt turn, Jahnavi confronted her, remarking, "Sometimes you reveal your true colors, a cunning woman who overlooks everything when it serves her purpose." As she departed, she left Divya with a lingering taunt, using the same word she had once hurled at her. Now, Divya eagerly awaits his arrival at the site.

When Aryan arrived later, he was directed to sit in the main area. While he sat silently, most of them focused on his appearance and style as he observed the arrangements. When he feels like it, he abruptly leaves without a word, much to everyone's complaints, and both Divya and Akanchha are powerless to do anything about it.

As he sits calmly one day, he notices his sister and other interns busy. He starts walking around, observing the arrangements. Gradually, he begins to examine the work, fixing any flaws, but reaches a point where he can't see the end of the blemish. Upon turning back, he noticed the door had abruptly closed and found himself in darkness. Suddenly, he received a text from an unknown number. "I hope you have a peaceful time enjoying yourself."

As he reads, he remains motionless until the gate unexpectedly unlocks hours later.

He angrily walks to the main area, stopping to scan the surroundings. Holding onto someone's hand, he takes her phone and reads the identical text that was sent to him. He angrily questioned, "Why did you deliberately lock me in that dark room that nobody ever visits?"

Jahnavi calmly responded to everyone's shocked expressions, explaining that she had to lock him in because he always leave without informing anyone. Our work is being hindered and both girls will remain silent towards you.

As he heard this, he quickly seized her by the neck, reminding her, "Be mindful of what you say about any of them." She calmly responded to his anger, "I was never scared of you, but now everyone is." Observing the fear in everyone's eyes, he loosened his grip and silently walked away.

Some time later, Akanchha and the other intern arrived at the scene, curious about the stunned reactions. Jahnavi enthusiastically informed everyone, "We had a productive discussion with Aryan, and he wholeheartedly promised to cooperate in our project without fail." Akanchha, who was searching for her sample, saw Jahnavi approaching her, holding it out. "There have been some changes in the plan," Jahnavi said, "so please work accordingly."

Looking at the sample, her eyes lit up with excitement as she saw the new concept applied in the plan, and she immediately began working on it. Meanwhile, Divya asked Jahnavi, her voice filled with concern, "What's the need to confine him in the dark room?"

"From today's lesson," she replied, "he will finally start taking our time and work seriously. It's all for him anyway, but he never seems concerned about it. That's why I have to take some action."

She was checking out other options when Divya told her, "I let you handle the project, but not him. So be careful before you do anything, it could make things worse."

"Does he still have a fear of the dark and his own solitude?" Jahnavi questioned. Paying no attention to her words, she walks away.

33
Chapter Thirty Three

Aryan arrives at the spot the following day and remains there longer while everyone carries out their tasks as expected. He stays quiet throughout every shot and only leaves when the work is finished. After reviewing some flawless solo shots of him, they have now progressed to the next stage, which involves a couple shots displaying grace and compatibility. This new idea has received positive feedback from everyone, but no one is willing to be his partner, whether they are staff, models, or even interns.

Akanchha appears tense observing everyone's peculiar behavior and decides to take a break to contemplate a solution. Aryan, sitting alone, spotted Jahnavi approaching him. He walked angrily towards her until she was cornered. She observed the anger in his eyes and fell silent, completely focused on him. Eventually, he left her alone.

Divya and the others are anxiously waiting for the new shoot result, as Akanchha appears to be missing from the spot. Following a moment of everyone rushing towards the main spot, Divya also made her way there. Upon arriving, she noticed a portrait of Jahnavi and Aryan that seemed perfect for a couple photoshoot, leaving Jahnavi and everyone else surprised and curious about how it came to be. Akanchha mentioned, "You're the only one who isn't afraid of my brother. I captured that sweet moment when you were talking to him."

Divya, while gazing at the portrait and a few other pictures of them, proclaimed that Jahnavi would now be the model for couple photoshoots before leaving for her cabin. All night, she sat alone in her cabin, fixated on the pictures, captivated by his unflinching eyes and the way she looked at him so lovingly, trying to understand her emotions in that moment.

When Aryan arrived at the spot the next day, he found his new costume and the prepared shooting location. He put on the suit and noticed that Jahnavi was wearing the matching costume. Upon witnessing this, he remains silent and proceeds to shoot discreetly at the location where his sister captured the recording. He spent a few days with her without speaking a word. One day, he looked at the dress, rejected it, and then walked over to the project sample. He asked for the pen after observing it. He took the pen from his sister, added new points and concepts, and silently handed it back to her.

While he was doing everything, he never glanced at his sister even once. Observing his quiet and composed demeanor, several models requested to shoot with him, each wearing a different outfit according to the theme, yet none of them matched him. Jahnavi, upon witnessing this, refrains from intervening, and eventually everyone departs from the scene.

Alone at the spot, he waits for the one and turns to admire the dress he picked. He admires her from head to toe, gently caressing her hand and exploring her heart, before placing his hand on her neck and feeling her pull him closer. He pulls her close by her waist, and she gazes at his lips, which appear thirsty. Then her eyes shift to his, but he remains fixated on her, consumed by desire.

She attempted to get off slowly, but when he noticed her leaving, he removed his own dress. Seeing this, she loosened the upper part of her dress. As a result, she stopped and took a step closer, where he attempted to touch her. However, upon seeing her resistance, he proceeded to remove his other dress and slowly took off her dress one by one. They gradually move closer to each other, until he stands half-naked by her side.

She realized there were no more options available, as they were too close, and he still looked at her with a longing gaze that she couldn't ignore any longer. He observed her longing for his emotions, and slowly handed her his diary, saying, "I want your feelings back, which seem absent from these pages," and departed.

After he departs that evening, he won't come back to the site where everyone seems tense because their project is only halfway completed. When they searched for previous details, they discovered that all their work had mysteriously vanished. Upon witnessing an unexpected event within the site, Jahnavi and others attempted to review the recording only to discover that all previous recordings had been deleted. Jahnavi walked into Divya's cabin, her eyes scanning the room for any signs of disorder. "What's happening here?" she asked, her voice filled with concern. "It looks like everything is missing from the site. This isn't how we do business."

Jahnavi noticed that she was silently listening to every word but not responding and saw that she was in a state where she seemed disconnected from herself. Disturbed, she silently leaves, leaving Divya alone on the site. As he glanced at his diary, memories of their last night together with Aryan came flooding back, when he urged her to express all her emotions. She is attempting to suppress her uncontrollable feelings for him by purposefully disappearing from work and deleting all records of their interactions.

34
Chapter Thirty Four

After a few days,

At college, Jahnavi confronts Divya, accusing her of intentionally deleting all recordings and site details.

Despite her silence, she asked her final question, "I don't understand why you did this, but it won't fix the already disastrous situation. All we can do is try, but if you choose to hold back, I won't push you."

As Jahnavi was leaving, Divya made a promise, "I will reimburse you for the amount you put into this project."

Jahnavi responded, "Let this be a positive debt in our little friendship," and departed.

Akanchha, who will never go back to college after that day, because all her work mysteriously disappeared, which was her only way to reconcile with her brother. Divya's absence still leaves her speechless as she grapples with how to fix things. Once again, she grabbed her sister's diary and reminisced about the moments Anjali and Akanchha shared as good friends, built on love and care that even Aryan couldn't deny.

On her way home, Akanchha unexpectedly pauses as she notices Divya's troop arriving to pick her up. Silently getting in the car, they brought her back to college. Upon arrival, she was surprised to see everyone waiting for her. As she reached the main ground, Divya approached and handed her a flower. Divya wished her a happy birthday and surprised her with a party she planned all by herself.

She hugged everyone around, expressing gratitude to those who still think of her. Despite the music, party, and gifts, she remained silent, gazing at the side of the college gate. As she stood at the gate, she finally smiled, but everyone else looked shocked as the guards stopped him from entering the college. Divya appeared annoyed when she glanced at the gate, but when Akanchha gently held her hand, she instructed the guards to open it. With a gift in hand, Aryan walked alongside Jahnavi towards the main area.

Arriving at the party, he presented the cake to her and handed her the knife, which she immediately used to cut it. He hands her a slice of his homemade cake and says, "Happy birthday, dear sister."

As she watched him standing in front of her, she struggled to find the right words to apologize. Meanwhile, he pulled out his phone and said, "I didn't have time to bring a gift, but I did manage to return your work, which only you have the right to own."

Saying this, he selected the option that launched the lost project on the company's portal, where everyone was amazed by his appearance and style. Everyone was suddenly shocked to see his couple shoot with Divya. When she saw the picture, she was shocked too. It was taken that night when no one else was present. So, who took the picture?

Finally, she recalls that he took the camera before leaving and now admires their perfect and beautiful pictures. Witnessing this, she directs her gaze towards the crowd, who shower her with praise for the shoot, as their bond and story captivate everyone's attention, fostering a feeling of connection when they view the picture. Jahnavi was taken aback when she saw the picture replaced by Divya's photo, causing her annoyance but maintained her silence.

Finally, Akanchha, who was aware that it wasn't her work, had the project named after her and received all the credit. However, when the reel was completed and everyone turned to cheer them on, Aryan vanished from the crowd as he came solely to give her the missing work. By doing this, he not only saved Divya from her project issue but also rescued the interns' work on the same project, before quietly leaving as a suspended student of the college.

After a month away from college, some of the work started up again, with ex-college staff and admin people returning, assisted by new interns and seniors. The security team was covertly handling the task until a few students suddenly lost consciousness. When they were brought to the hospital, all of them were diagnosed with drug use, with most of them in critical condition.

Going forward, college is now facing regular issues, such as money laundering and kidnapping, with many college students involved in illegal activities led by the college administration. Divya, unaware of everything, found herself trapped in personal issues until she discovered unfamiliar activities. Before she could react, a group of unidentified students appeared. Upon arriving at the college, they enforced strict security measures and began searching for something, while the leader of the group awaited the opening of a long-sealed secret chamber.

35

Chapter Thirty Five

As soon as Divya found out about this, she immediately commanded her armed forces to intervene. With the assistance of a tracker and college security, the head of the mob discovered the hidden chamber. Upon opening it, he discovered a stockpile of ammunition and drugs. He quickly gave the order to load the trucks. Once everything was loaded, they began to leave. However, they encountered a locked main gate. They then made their way towards another exit post, only to find it sealed as well.

Upon witnessing this, he requested to inspect the stocked inventory, but received no response. Then, he held a few students hostage and headed towards another exit. As he reached there, he noticed armed forces moving in to rescue the college.

Noticing he was trapped, he drove recklessly, leading the crew to the other exit where some members got separated, and finally reached the last exit where he found only one guard. Despite almost reaching his destination, he refused to open the gate, resulting in a severe collision that caused the vehicle to lose balance. Injured students slowly exit the vehicle, while the leader emerges with the hostage, attempting to escape.

Noticing the lone guard ahead, he was taken aback and swiftly pointed his gun at him. Surrounded by his crew, uttered, "It's been ages since I last checked my supplies, but you've helped me recover them. Take one for yourself."

He seemed annoyed as he took the package again, reminded of the mess he created because of this drug. Despite his efforts to avoid it, he couldn't help but notice that his unique friend's college was in danger again. Overcome with emotion, he instinctively grabbed his neck.

Despite being annoyed, his crew attacks him without causing any pain. He fights back, breaking them all as he forcefully takes them to the main ground. He loaded himself onto his own truck, started the ignition, and began driving recklessly, running over his crew, other vehicles, and destroying the stuff they had collected. In the process, he didn't see anyone coming in between, and to save them all, they all gathered at one place.

Despite everything, he refuses to stop, and only when he realizes there's no escape, he abandons the moving truck to join his crew at a specific location. He caused a severe collision, resulting in the death of nearly everyone, as he anxiously checks if the crew leader survived. He is now being apprehended by armed forces and taken into custody. When he sees the former Manager of this college, who is now the head of the mob and almost destroyed the college last time, he intervenes with him. Now, with the same incident happening again, he is about to attack him upon seeing him alive.

Out of the injured hostage, a girl suddenly grabs his hand and whispers, "Save yourself."

While uttering these words, she passed out and collapsed into his arms. Seeing his sister in a worse condition, he becomes uncontrollable. He swiftly drew his gun and shot at the mob, but security intervened just in time to save them. Unfortunately, the bullet accidentally struck the truck, causing a massive explosion that destroyed everything they had gathered. With their vehicle engulfed in flames, they had no choice but to surrender and were subsequently seized by the armed forces.

36
Chapter Thirty Six

Aryan looks disoriented while carrying his sister. Divya arrived at the site with her staff and caught Aryan in the act, leading to the arrest of everyone by the police and security. Immediately, she grabbed the gun from his hand, and just as they approached, a team of lawyers and high officials arrived with prepared legal documents to protect Aryan from the legal actions.

As he left with his injured sister, people noticed his savage look but didn't hate him this time because they understood his pain. Divya, gripping his gun, remained motionless and watched him silently as he left, unable to intervene because this time he wouldn't allow anyone near him, not even his well-wisher. She is now faced with the reality of the worst things she had only read in her sister's diary, as she stares at the gun adorned with an antique emblem. When she saw the emblem, she appeared shocked at how he obtained the gun, and then she met with the white-collar individuals who were still handling college affairs.

Upon asking, she discovers that her sister had hired a special team to protect Aryan in times of trouble. The head of the armed forces approached Divya and gave her all the details about the incident. As he was leaving, he noticed the gun in her hand and appeared terrified. He then asked her, "Where did you get this gun?"

Yet, when she appeared silent, he hesitantly took it from her and passed it to the special team to correctly position it. Upon regaining her senses, she noticed the elite team - highly trained and equipped with the same ancient emblem, representing the secret force of her parent company that had remained concealed from her until now.

Right away, she took back the gun and stated that she would keep it safe until it could be delivered to its rightful owner, permitting everyone else to go for the time being.

Even though they are listening to her, they refuse to leave until they see her legal documentation. She confidently displayed her legal documentation proving her ownership of the company, causing the head of the force to reluctantly declare, "We will temporarily retreat, but we will come back to reclaim this weapon."

Divya, who was taken aback by the unexpected events today, questioned why Aryan had a gun. Why does her security team appear terrified when they see this antique gun and its emblem? What makes it special and what kind of power does it possess? Furthermore, who is this new regiment that only emerged upon hearing this gunshot?

She appears agitated thinking about everything, then she sets the gun down and heads to Aryan's house. Upon arrival, her personal doctor was waiting for her and provided all the details. "Ma'am, everything is under control as she has already received treatment and will recover soon. However, we need to monitor her mental state as she appears to be in shock from today's incident. We will all remain here to take care and keep you updated."

She stood at the gate of the cursed house, lacking the courage to enter, and quietly left without seeing Akanchha. Meanwhile, Aryan takes care of his sister at home and remains silent for a few days until his mother calls to inquire about their well-being. Upon witnessing his sister's unconscious state, he calmly assured, "She's just engrossed in a college project, which I'm also helping with. We'll head home once we finish. Don't worry." With that, he ended the call and patiently waited for her to regain consciousness.

37

Chapter Thirty Seven

During weekend, Aryan would sneak into the college and head straight to the secret chamber. Upon arrival, he revealed the protected truck that he stored in the basement. As he observed the stocks, he briefly glanced around the basement and discovered everything was new. Upon seeing this, he walks towards the dark room and is shocked to find new stock filled inside, which he had already burned.

Wondering how they managed to make it work even after he destroyed everything last time. As he gazes at the truck filled with cargo, he ponders why it hasn't been taken away and why it was left open as if inviting him to enter once more. When he reaches this point, he becomes attentive as if there is someone else with him. There, he notices the former manager walking anxiously. Just as he is about to approach him, the manager collapses and hands him a note.

"You have what you desired. May you halt what you unknowingly started?"

In the meantime, Dean hurriedly made his way to a secluded corner of the college campus, where he found a door and unlocked it. Upon entering, he was confronted with the sight of the main accused, who had been securely tied up. Seeing this, his face tensed up as he spotted Aryan nearby.

About to lose his composure, he demanded that Dean seal off a section of the college, vowing no one would leave until he had his revenge. Just as he was about to leave, he paused and cautioned, "Son, trying to conquer an army with bare hands is impossible."

Disregarding what he said, Aryan heads home; but upon reaching his house, he stops and looks back, only to find Jahnavi following him. He stayed silent and quietly entered his house, shutting the gate in her face.

When Aryan opens the door for the doctor who comes to his house for checkups on alternate days, he notices a suspicious car parked nearby. Upon noticing it, he approached and found the car unlocked. He proceeded to open the gate and searched for the car owner's details. Before he could react, the car unexpectedly locked itself. Looking ahead, he noticed Jahnavi, who purposefully locked him and proceeded to enter the house after the doctor.

Aryan sat and waited until the car got unlocked. Once it did, he entered his house. As he reached the room, he noticed Jahnavi sitting near his sister, holding her hand with care and talking to her while she rested. The doctor said she's alright, but it would be beneficial for her to spend time with loved ones to help alleviate her stress.

Aryan slowly approaches her side as she regains consciousness, but this time she remains silent, unlike her usual self, leaving him unable to provide support. Even though he was present, he couldn't prevent her from getting hurt, and the incident is still vivid in his memory. Upon thinking this, he immediately exits the room, leaving Jahnavi behind for the entire day. When it grew late, Aryan returned to find Jahnavi resting in the chair, still holding Akanchha's hand. Witnessing this, he carefully placed her next to her sister to rest, then silently left, patiently awaiting the arrival of the next day.

38

Chapter Thirty Eight

The next day,

When Jahnavi woke up, she appeared slightly frightened upon seeing Aryan waiting. She emerges from his house, where he was waiting by her car, noticing his tired and dazed eyes as if he hadn't slept all night. He opens the gate slowly for her. However, before getting into the car, she pauses and expresses gratitude for letting her stay with her only friend who still needs support to recover soon. Instantly, she embraced him, but he didn't react, and she expressed, "I wish I could understand the pain you're experiencing."

As she was about to leave, he reached out and asked, "Will you stay with her longer?"

Upon hearing this, she shuts the car door and opens the trunk. Upon seeing this, he retreats to the spot where he noticed her luggage, packed and ready to move in, realizing she had already planned everything. He then carried her luggage directly to Akanchha's room, where he noticed a smile on her face before he left. Once Jahnavi finally entered her house as planned, she calmly sat down to prepare for her next move.

Aryan patiently waits for his sister's recovery, refusing to rest until she is better, while Jahnavi takes care of all her needs. Jahnavi appears composed while visiting his sister in intensive care, but when he enters the main room, he notices Aryan constantly checking the clock and scanning the door as if expecting someone.

Yet, he observes no one arriving, he silently departs.

One night, while Akanchha appeared to be resting, she walked over to Aryan's room where he was sitting idle. Standing next to him, she remarked, "It's been a while since you've rested." With drowsy eyes, he glanced at her, and she gently helped him lie on the bed, where he gradually drifted off to sleep. As she moves closer, she gazes at his peacefully closed eyes and his hand that clings to her as if he's still afraid of the dark. Witnessing this, she feels fortunate that her presence won't cause him any pain this time.

Upon waking up, Aryan seems irritated, wondering how he was able to fall asleep. He reaches the other room and sees her engaged in a video call, with Akanchha responding as well. Observing this, he takes a step back, and after a while, Jahnavi moves to the kitchen to start preparing something. But she stops at one moment and watches him from a distance, marveling at how effortlessly he is cooking. "You appear to be in a good mood today," she remarked after seeing him calm for the first time in a while. Upon hearing this, he questioned, "Who were you talking to my sister with?"

"Only a couple of friends," she replied nonchalantly. He turned towards her side and said, "I only want her loved ones by her side, no one else."

She answered, "So, why don't you stay with her? Is it your ego that still prevents you from even inquiring about her well-being?"

After hearing this, he said, "Your main job is to watch over my sister, so you don't have to worry about me anymore."

As he was leaving, she questioned, "Why can't you easily let go of the past? You can only see the present then."

Upon hearing this, he responds angrily, "I will always remember the day when my sister got hurt, even though I was there, I couldn't protect her, and I will never forget it as long as I live."

When he shares his pain with her, she quietly listens and then departs, while Aryan, annoyed, keeps recalling the incident repeatedly. Filled with anger, he refuses to show himself to anyone, while Jahnavi, who hasn't seen him since that day, becomes anxious and attempts to go to his room.

When she reached there, she saw him lying unconscious on the bed, prompting her to run towards him. When she touched his body, it felt like it was burning. As she looked around, she noticed a package of drugs. Not knowing what to do, she called emergency services and waited for help to arrive. Eventually, when it arrived, she left him alone with the person who will care for him. It had been a while since Jahnavi sat silently beside Akanchha. Suddenly, a memory flashed in her mind - the moment when she touched Aryan and felt his tight grip, as if they were one body. In that moment, she could sense his longing for her love.

Unable to contain her emotions any longer, she kissed him passionately, and in that moment, he responded with an untamed desire while she tenderly cared for him. He treated her with a wild and rude intensity, alternating between inflicting pain and pleasure upon her, leaving her helpless before his insatiable desires that only seemed to grow stronger. In the end, she realized there was no other way to appease him than to surrender herself to him physically.

"My well-wisher, I need you," Aryan whispered slowly.

Upon hearing someone else's name, she gently disentangled herself from his embrace and turned to face him, tears welling up in her eyes, witnessing his longing for the care of his well-wisher despite his own pain. As she witnessed his deteriorating condition, she finally picked up the phone and called Divya, urgently requesting her to come over.

39

Chapter Thirty Nine

Once Divya arrives, Jahnavi discreetly leaves the room, leaving them alone. Divya administers the antidote to reduce his drugged state. Meanwhile, Jahnavi, in the main area, appears anxious about his health. Unable to wait any longer, she heads towards Aryan's room. Upon arrival, she was taken aback to witness them engaged in a passionate moment. In response, she quietly closed the gate and proceeded to Akanchha's room, patiently waiting until she finished attending to Aryan.

At dawn,

Jahnavi, who had been waiting, finally saw Divya standing before her. Without asking anything, Divya slowly held Akanchha's hand and apologized for everything. It was Divya's mistake that caused her to bring Aryan back, but in doing so, she lost them both. Divya's selfishness caused harm to Akanchha, who had trusted her deeply. Jahnavi, who couldn't bear it any longer, then told her to leave. As she listens, she approaches and takes her hand, gently tracing a path from her heart to her neck, revealing the marks Aryan left on her body.

While glancing at the marks, Divya reminded her of their arrangement - she would provide him with the remaining shares, but only if Aryan perceived her as a well-wisher and not as the businesswoman who had caused harm to his sister. "I need you to shoulder all the blame and avoid being around Akanchha. If you stay close to her, he will also form a connection with you, which I don't want. Finish the work you came for so we can close the deal successfully." Saying this, Divya left.

Jahnavi, who remains silent despite listening to her words, thinking how Divya now seeks to ruin her only relationship with Akanchha, as her sole focus is on Aryan. But now she is powerless to act, having already made a deal with Divya.

When Aryan wakes up, he immediately looks at the drug package he's holding and checks to see if he did something strange. Everything seemed fine, but then he tried to recall what happened last night. He only remembers seeing Jahnavi, who came looking for him. After that, he has no memory, so he decides to investigate further.

Upon entering the room, he observed that only Akanchha was present, resting. Noticing his sister alone, he approaches and takes a seat beside her, and eventually she regains awareness. Upon seeing this, he glanced to her side where she attempted to sit. He offered his assistance and they both sat in silence, finally locking eyes after a long while. After some time, she attempted to communicate with him, but he interrupted her, saying, "Just let me know if I'm on the right track, whatever it is you want."

Despite her agreement, Aryan struggles to understand what she wants and when she wants it, making him feel like a failure. Finally, he approaches her and gently takes her hand, saying, "I wish I could comprehend your deepest desires. However, if I were in your position, I would prioritize eating first, as it requires considerable strength to recover from my own weakness."

As he speaks, she slowly agrees and he smiles at her, leading her to the dining room where she calmly watches him prepare food. Afterwards, he has her try it and shortly after, he starts preparing something else. This cycle continues throughout the entire day, and in doing so, they both seem happy, reliving the old times that he had almost forgotten while being away from his family. Finally, he embraced his sister and guided her back to her room, ensuring she fell asleep before returning to the main room and waiting for

Jahnavi's arrival.

At night,

Jahnavi, who arrives at night, caught sight of him patiently waiting for her. As she slowly set down the belongings on the dining table, she noticed numerous dishes but disregarded them all. Heading towards the room, he questioned, "Can you please tell me where you were and why you left without informing me? At the very least, you should consider her before leaving."

She interrupted him, saying, "I left you both to get together, as my presence was no longer needed." While leaving, she ignored Aryan's request to try his dishes and headed towards the room. Aryan, upon witnessing this, chooses not to speak and walks away. Jahnavi, who was sitting with Akanchha, appears lost until she remembers last night, causing her eyes to well up with emotion. "We might cause you inconvenience this time," Akanchha said in a shaky voice, "but I can't take care of my brother by myself. I need my best friend to assist me with this responsibility."

As she listened to her words after a long time, she immediately hugged her, tears welling up in her eyes, unwilling to part from her for some time. Once she regained her composure, she appeared calm and deliberately erased all the painful memories, now solely concentrating on Akanchha's well-being, completely disregarding Aryan's presence or anything associated with him. She only comes when he's gone.

Meanwhile, Aryan, who's seeing his sister getting better, wants to spend more time with her but can't because Jahnavi ignores him. However, he's willing to put up with it for the sake of his sister's well-being. Then one day, he hands her a note saying, "I want some time with my sister, and I want you to be there too." She reads it and walks out of the room. Aryan entered the room and spent the entire day bonding with his sister. As he was about to leave after putting her to sleep, he noticed Jahnavi standing at the doorstep, who had been there since he moved in.

Although she wasn't physically present, she witnessed everything and surprisingly enjoyed her time with them. When he tried to ask her about it, she ignored him and walked into another room. Aryan, who was calm after seeing his sister well, became tense again when he thought about Jahnavi's strange behavior. Despite her inability to stand him even for a moment, she continues to reside in the same house. Reflecting on what went wrong, he realizes he can't remember anything from the previous events once she starts taking care of him, and she acts strangely after that night.

She used to enjoy his company, but now she avoids him wherever he goes. Aryan lies down on the bed, trying to recall more, and as he closes his eyes, he sees fragments of that night when he and Jahnavi grew closer. He abruptly woke up from his slumber and now appears anxious upon learning about that night.

Aryan waits in the main area for Jahnavi, who arrives after seeing his text. Aryan immediately stated, "You have been taking care of my sister for a long time. I want you to leave us alone now."

As she quietly left while he spoke, he suggested, "You should let her know you're leaving today and won't be coming back."

Her eyes welled up with tears as she listened, but he paid no attention and now he waits. Jahnavi went to Akanchha's room and later emerged holding her belongings, ready to leave. However, before departing, she glanced around the house and, in the end, looked at him, but he didn't acknowledge her presence. In response to his silence, she quietly left his house, just as he had desired.

40

Chapter Forty

After a few weeks,

Akanchha, who had been away from college for a long time, was welcomed back with excitement. As soon as she entered the campus, she was accompanied by armed forces for protection. Upon seeing this, she turned and noticed Divya standing there. Divya immediately hugged her and said, "I feel blessed seeing you fine." After expressing her gratitude, she then inquired about her early arrival at college.

Just as she was about to speak, Aryan's return to college left everyone in shock. More armed forces seemed to be supporting him as he entered the campus. Akanchha, suspicious, asked Divya why there was so much security around them.

Divya replied, "for your safety."

Upon hearing this, she immediately turns towards her brother who had come to pick her up. "As you wish," he said, his voice filled with resignation. "I let you come in here, but now it's time to leave."

He was leaving, and Akanchha watched him go, her eyes filled with a mix of sadness and nostalgia. Divya holds her hand and says, "I'll take you home because I want to spend more time with you," and Aryan is reminded of someone who once asked the same question. While contemplating, he glanced at Akanchha and said, "I'll be there to pick you up when it's time to leave. Take care of yourself until then."

Divya, who anxiously waits and watches until he leaves, revealing her deep insecurity for him, Akanchha immediately says, "I know why you stopped me. You only care about my brother, and no one else." Shocked, Divya turns to her side. Continuing her statement, Akanchha said, "When you visited me, I heard you talking to Jahnavi. However, I fell asleep because I was drugged, so I only caught that you want him to come back to this college and that you sent Jahnavi to take care of me."

Divya remains unruffled after realizing she was only aware of half the truth. Akanchha then asked, "Can you please let me know where our other partner is? I have a few things to discuss with her as well."

Divya then saw Jahnavi approaching Akanchha, signaling her to stay hidden. Seeing this, Jahnavi abruptly halts, allowing Divya to swiftly whisk Akanchha away. While sitting alone, Akanccha asked, "Did you finish the project?"

Divya then holds her hand calmly, as she says, "it would never be completed until it's not approved by our lead photographer."

Akanchha appeared calm, but there was a silent tension in her demeanor. Divya, observing this, inquired, "Would you like to take charge of the assignment this time?"

She feels helpless, saying, "He won't accept this offer after what happened before."

Divya delicately holds her hand, pausing the conversation abruptly, "I've burdened you enough, but no more after this." They both sit peacefully, admiring the beauty of nature. Jahnavi feels calm as she watches them from afar, but when she sees them leaving, she also wants to leave. As she turns, she accidentally collides with an unknown person.

Divya and Akanchha glanced at the clock and exclaimed, "It's time to go." They moved forward and witnessed Aryan supporting Jahnavi to prevent her from falling. Aryan patiently waited for his sister, and that's when Akanchha finally met Jahnavi. Without any questions, Jahnavi hugged her and expressed how glad she was to see her again, suggesting they spend some time together. When she said this, Akanchha held both girls' hands and looked at Aryan, requesting a little more time.

Upon seeing his sister's wish, he suggested, "Why not invite them to our house? It's been a while since we last met our parents."

Saying this, he appears quiet, while everyone's gaze shifts towards Aryan, who seems lost in conversation about home. Jahnavi grabs Akanchha's hand and declares, "She's coming with me." As they all departed, Aryan glanced back and noticed a new bench placed in that exact spot where he met his unique friend. Carefully touching it, he looked ahead to his precious spot, which he had nearly forgotten to visit. As he gazed upon the breathtaking nature that he had spent countless hours exploring with his unique friend, a sense of longing washed over him, as if he were searching for something he had lost. Gradually, he began to regain his senses, only to realize that there was someone standing nearby. "It's a little gift for your returning," Divya said, her words filled with hope, "may you start again with a fresh start."

Upon hearing this, Aryan slowly turns towards Divya, who is leaving without making eye contact as if she is still afraid of him. When Jahnavi and Akanchha arrived home, Divya also arrived shortly after. Aryan's mother greeted them all with a smile upon seeing the visitors. Jahnavi appeared to be fully immersed with Aryan's family and was enjoying her time effortlessly, while Divya, who came solely because of Aryan, desired to explore the house and was wandering around in search of something.

She finally reached Aryan's room, unlocked it, and entered. In that place, she experienced both loneliness and unspoken words that remained trapped inside the room. She had been there for a while, but as she left and reached the main area, she saw everyone gathered in the garden area, all looking happy and smiling. As she observes them in one place, his final words come back to her: "It's been a long meeting with parents."

Noticing his empty spot, she desires to fill the void, when suddenly someone grabs her hand from behind and leads her to the garden. Divya silently followed his lead and joined the group without uttering a word.

Everyone appears excited to see Aryan, but his mother seems particularly emotional after not seeing him for a long time. He holds his mother gently, appearing lost as if he has missed his family dearly. Witnessing their reunion, everyone feels blessed, making the moment precious. Both girls requested to leave after enjoying a great time with the Aryan family, to which Aryan calmly responded, "Why not stay for dinner? My mother doesn't like it when people leave on an empty stomach, so please stay!"

As Aryan prepares dinner, the sounds of sizzling and chopping echo through the room, building anticipation for the meal to come. Aryan, who hadn't spoken to Jahnavi all day, gently handed her a small gift, his hand trembling with care. "Thank you for sharing the precious moment with my family," he whispered. Jahnavi accepted the gift in silence, then quietly left with her driver. Divya was finally preparing to leave, but not before she exhausted every effort to persuade Aryan about the proposal, only to find herself helpless and now compelled to depart. Akanchha, who had resigned herself to her fate, finally mustered the strength to express gratitude for everything.

41

Chapter Forty One

—♡—

While in the process of moving to her villa, Divya abruptly came to a stop, her gaze fixed on Aryan standing by the car. With a calm demeanor, he warned her, "It's too late for you to be outside."

Believing he would let her continue to her villa, she quickly realizes she can't let that happen and abruptly changes the car's direction towards his cursed house. Upon reaching there, she silently gets out of her car and enters his house. Aryan follows her lead, noticing her waiting for him at the main area. Standing so close, she could feel his heartbeat against her own chest, but she remained silent. He carefully read her lips and pleaded, "Please stay tonight."

He couldn't wait any longer, so he scooped her up in his arms, feeling her legs wrap around his waist, and held her tightly by her shoulders as they made their way to his room. With each step he took, she felt herself getting lost in thoughts of the passionate night they had spent together. Eventually, she couldn't resist anymore and began kissing him softly on his neck, until she couldn't hold back any longer and sensually bit him. This led them both to the bed, consumed by desire. She refuses to hold back, revealing all her desires and how desperately she craves him on this solitary night.

In the late morning, Aryan is still sleeping, but Divya is wide awake and everything appears normal, as if nothing happened the night before. She attempted to recall the moment she surrendered herself, and Aryan embraced her tightly to soothe her longings, while he continued to apologize and care for her. To suppress her growing desires, he holds onto her, but he never stops caring for her; instead, he accepts everything she brings, and finally, she appears calm as she was leaving.

Once again, he pulls her closer, afraid she will leave. Observing his peaceful sleep, she remains by his side, longing to sleep next to him. Aryan woke up in the evening and found himself in her arms, still peacefully asleep. Upon seeing this, he decides not to disturb her and quietly gets out of bed. He then goes downstairs to prepare something for her. While he is cooking, he catches glimpses of the dark night and whispers, "I need you." He appears startled, but tries to remember more clearly this time, only to see blurry glimpses before his eyes.

He faces the mirror, observing himself as if he had been the one who asked someone to spend the night with him. He recalls the previous night and slowly removes his shirt, revealing marks all over his body that were given to him by his well-wisher. He remembers every mark her lips left on him, always filled with longing. Despite the marks, he tries to remember that night and that person. While lost in thought, he hears something and rushes to get dressed and go outside. Aryan noticed Divya leaving without saying goodbye, making him worried about what is still hurting her despite their closeness.

42

Chapter Forty Two

On the next day,

Aryan, who had finally returned to college, went straight to Divya's room and found her working calmly. He placed the phone that she had forgotten at his house the day before on the desk. She took her phone and saw that Akanchha had sent her picture of an emotional moment of Aryan and his mother. As she gazed at the mesmerizing scene before her, it seemed like she was transported into another world for a brief moment. "Start fresh on a positive tone," he said. Continuing with the same lines, he then added, "Are you still working on that project, the one where my sister got injured?"

Divya, who appeared contemplative for a moment, gently grasps the picture in her hand and approaches, displaying it before him. "You seem stuck in the past, but I envision a vibrant future that only your younger sister can rewrite. It's you who's holding her back." As he listened, he released everything and gently held her, urging her to meet his gaze as he said, "You must decide between me and my future."

Divya, without hesitation, responded, "I prioritize your future and saving both you and this college. I hope you won't object this time." Aryan, feeling trapped, sees no alternative but to go there; he glances at the picture once more before departing.

In the garden, he observes his sister sitting quietly, no longer expressing her interests or desires. Noticing her reserved demeanor, he invites her to sit next to him and shows her the picture she had already shared with Divya. He then asks, "Is there anything you would like to talk about with me?"

He gently takes her hand as she hesitates, reassuring her, "I'm not the same person you see at college. I'll always be your big brother, trying to make you happy. If this is truly what you want, I'll support you. May it bring a smile back to your face."

Divya and the rest of the staff were going to the meeting room, where they found Akanchha waiting with the prepared presentation for the next campaign. As she returned, everyone's excitement grew, but before the meeting began, Akanchha requested to call Jahnavi, prompting Divya to order an immediate call.

Jahnavi joined the meeting and Akanchha presented the new theme and campaign blueprint to everyone. The majority likes it, except for Jahnavi who disagrees. Divya requested everyone to carry on with the assignment as she maintains her position of authority. Everyone resumed their work after listening to her, and Jahnavi left without saying anything. Now, only Akanchha and Divya remained in the meeting room. Akanchha appeared worried when she saw Jahnavi's strange behavior, while Divya was still curious about how she convinced Aryan. "He came up to me and specifically asked that I redo the assignment," she replied.

Divya joyfully exclaimed, "At last, he made your wish come true."

In response, Akanchha said, "He wasn't the one who did it; he was compelled to." Divya appears quiet after hearing this. Akanchha expressed, "I've already lost my brother, so now we're just siblings in name, as everyone knows. The day I signed this contract, everything changed. I got hurt, and on that very same day, I lost my beloved brother. His absence left a void, and he had always been against me taking on this assignment. But now, I am back at this college, trying to uncover the reason behind his actions."

With that said, she walks away, leaving Divya to ponder while smiling to herself, thinking, "You'll never be able to find that person."

Akanchha, sitting in the same spot when Jahnavi joins her. "Why are you opposing me this time?" Akanchha asked.

She replied, "Certain emotions are so valuable that they must be safeguarded from others, otherwise they lose their significance. If I were in your position, I would have preserved them in my memories, untouched by anyone."

Akanchha replied, "One day, you'll appreciate the decision I'm making, even though you're not by my side now. But in the future, you'll be a part of it." Jahnavi reassured her, "I've never doubted you and will always support your decisions."

Jahnavi witnessed Aryan leaving discreetly, but she chose to ignore him and they both continued working silently. Later, Akanchha noticed Aryan waiting for her and he safely escorted her home.

Despite everything going according to plan, Divya is at a loss on how to approach him due to the main part not working. She must get him to work on her major plan for it to come to fruition. As she contemplates how to approach him, she strolls around the college campus. She comes across the backside of the garden and halts at one point, where she delicately touches his charred bike. He destroyed the gift from her sister in a last-ditch attempt to bring her back into his life.

When she looks at it, she feels an overwhelming sense of love, as if there were no boundaries between them. She called her trusted staff, instructing them to prepare the gift with care. With a smile on her face, she thought to herself, "As promised, a new story of Aryan and Divya will unfold, written by my own hand, and he must accept it."

While leaving college with Akanchha, Aryan spotted Divya standing ahead of him but he continued walking. Asking him, she said, "You seem to be too concerned about your sister's safety, don't you?"

Aryan stops abruptly, and moments later a group of security personnel arrive, summoned by Divya. "From now on, they will be responsible for Akanchha's safety," Divya declares firmly, emphasizing her commitment to protecting the lead photographer of their campaign.

Divya has designated a company car for Akanchha's safe commute to and from her residence. As soon as Aryan sees this, he lets Akanchha go in. Divya added, "because of your consistent tardiness and your role as the lead model for our campaign, our company has also provided you with a company vehicle. This will help us expedite our work."

She turns her head and spots the sleek, newly modified bike, prompting him to walk towards it. His hand grazed the bike gently, savoring the sensation of the cool metal beneath his fingertips. He then paused, his mind wandering to something deep in thought. He suggested, "Maybe there was an error when they assigned me this bike? It's too costly."

Divya's words were clear and unwavering as she stated, "I never make a mistake when it comes to you. Accept this small gift from me as a token of my appreciation."

Reluctantly, she handed him the keys, but he still refused to take them, causing her to say, "Let's begin anew on a positive note. These keys are a gift from your well-wisher, and it will bring you joyful memories that won't cause any pain."

Hearing the same word of his 'unique friend', but this time it was his well-wisher who knowingly gave it to him as a gift. Silently, he took the keys from her hand, causing an immediate calmness to settle among everyone. Everyone else was leaving, leaving only Aryan and Divya, who locked eyes but felt no previous emotions or connection. As he accepts her gift, he notices her calmness and then rides away on his bike. As she watches him depart, she smiles, knowing he still cares for her unconditionally and supports her because of a promise made to his well-wisher, a promise she will utilize to regain everything she lost, ensuring he remains in her life.

Akanchha, who remains calm while working on her new assignment, suddenly recalls something from the past and interrupts her current work to search for her previous work. She searched for it but couldn't find it anywhere, so she ended up retrieving her camera from her brother. Upon reviewing the specifics, she realized it was devoid of any content, as he had extracted all the information from it. She appeared tense, wondering why he erased all the details informing no one, and why no one questioned him.

She searched for Jahnavi, but couldn't find her, so she went to the CEO's cabin. While searching for information, she eventually came across pictures of Aryan and Divya that he had already shared on the company portal. She started going through them and paused at a certain point where he had not posted much. Divya had kept those pictures to herself and never mentioned them.

While examining the details, she stumbled upon the contract Aryan signed with a rival company to deliver the three compositions. Despite the date having already passed, nothing has been done. This realization makes her anxious. Her brother is always doing things for others, including the college, but never seeks recognition. She wonders who he goes through all this trouble for.

Aryan, upon leaving his class, made his way to the restricted section. When he arrives, he encounters Dean, who was already waiting for him. Without uttering a word, Aryan proceeded to torture the main accused, defying the Dean's attempts to stop him. By pushing him away and yelling, "If you continue torturing him, he will die. What will you do then? Do you want to graduate from this college as a murderer or do you truly care about your future? Everyone is giving their utmost effort for your sake. You do not possess the right to destroy their efforts, so I kindly request that you cease your actions and redirect your attention towards completing your responsibilities."

Aryan shouted, "Nobody is allowed to leave this college, and I no longer care about my future. My only concern is seeking revenge and locating the mastermind behind this drug scam." He begins torturing him until he loses consciousness. "Thank you for taking care of this culprit," he finally said, "as we still have many things to resolve."

43

Chapter Forty Three

Jahnavi had been noticing Aryan's suspicious behavior for the past few days, but she kept her observations to herself. While leaving one day, he noticed Jahnavi looking tense and followed her. He saw her enter a room. He enters the room, just like she did, only to find it's a dance rehearsal room. Everyone is dancing with a partner, except for her. No one dares to be near her since that incident. Witnessing her vulnerability, he was about to leave, but he reconsidered and approached her. Standing at the front, he watched as everyone silently filed out of the room, including her, who left without uttering a word.

Curious about her sudden change in behavior towards him, he yearned to uncover the exact reason behind her actions. From that day on, no one ever appeared in the rehearsal room whenever Aryan arrived. Seeing this, Jahnavi stormed angrily to the rehearsal room, only to find Aryan waiting for her. He gently took her hand and led her to dance. Instead of speaking to him, she silently engaged in dancing with him and when he finished, he left silently. Jahnavi, taken aback by his peculiar actions, left pondering why he unexpectedly appeared and offered to help her.

Since that day, Aryan, who is now composed, no longer attends rehearsals, instead exploring the campus in search of something unknown to others. The college's main stud, who constantly watches and follows him, seized the perfect chance to enter a restricted area when Aryan didn't show up one day. Upon reaching the basement, he discovered a stash of drugs, which brought him satisfaction as he now had something to seek revenge with. Following this, he discreetly arranged his small team to distribute the drug to different sectors.

Akanchha goes straight to Divya, when she gets no answer, demanding all the hidden details. Divya remains silent when shown the details.

Divya, without uttering a word, was about to leave when Jahnavi grabbed her hand, questioning, "What is happening? Why were we kept in the dark about all this? Is there anything else that you're keeping hidden from us?"

Realizing there was no way out, Divya hesitated before uttering the words. "We're completely stuck, and the only solution is to bring back former Aryan. But I can't do it without your assistance."

She presented the blueprint of her major project that she had been working on for the past few months. Akanchha's eyes widened in shock as she realized the truth. "You purposely suspended him to buy yourself time to plan everything for his career advancement without him suspecting your secret involvement. While doing this, you willingly bear the weight of his anger upon yourself."

Divya answered, her voice filled with determination, "He has already done so much for this college, but we still need him back to save our college's reputation. Furthermore, his career needs to be secured. If I have to hurt him again in order to achieve this, I won't hesitate to do so."

Akanchha held her tight, her voice filled with gratitude as she said, "You truly care for my brother. If it's not you, no one else could look after him like you did. And in this, we stand by your side."

Jahnavi, who understood her intentions, held hands with Divya while feeling tense about her actions, as she cleverly manipulated everything in her favor, unbeknownst to Akanchha.

Aryan, completely oblivious to what was happening behind him, was busy preparing for something significant, until he suddenly came to a halt on his way. He slowly turned to the other side and noticed a group of students distributing drugs to different people. Despite wanting to intervene, he restrained himself upon seeing his sister waiting for him on the other side.

He approaches his sister as she requested him to be present at the shoot tomorrow, at the same time. He agreed and as soon as she left, he made another attempt to chase the drug suppliers, but by then they had all vanished from the scene. As he turned to leave, he saw the admin staff handing him an official notice, which stated that they were initiating a first warning on him for missing classes and being absent from the working site. Ignoring the letter, he resumes his secret work and remains unaffected by anything that could hinder his studies.

44

Chapter Forty Four

Aryan has been absent from every location for the past few days, and before his shoot, he goes to the restricted area, where he is being followed by an unknown person. After arriving at the secret room, he calmly inquires about the main traitor's identity, but the person remains silent. Observing this, he refrains from asking any more questions, silently providing food. Once the person is full, he resumes torturing them until they lose consciousness.

By doing this daily, he experiences a sense of calm. However, as he was leaving, he noticed that Jahnavi, who had been following him all the way, stopped. Seeing his hand covered in blood, she approach cautiously to examine the cut. While standing nearby, she unexpectedly caught sight of the main culprit, who was covered in blood. Seeing this, she appeared shocked, especially since his hand was currently covered in his blood. Without any questions, she promptly leaves upon witnessing this. Aryan, who appeared silent at that moment, finally witnessed her fear of him for the first time. With this thought, he glanced at the clock and then left the spot for the shoot.

When Aryan arrived at the campaign site, he found it empty except for his sister waiting for him. Spotting him, she swiftly started her work, completely alone. Recognizing her commitment, he silently helps her with the shoot as she desires.

Aryan peacefully sits on the bench, enjoying the scenic beauty, when he notices a notebook placed there. Upon taking it, he discovered it was the syllabus he had fallen behind on. He looked around but saw no one there. He proceeded to take out his book and diligently completed his syllabus.

Aryan joined the lecture while everyone else was already attending and calmly stayed until it ended. As everyone was leaving, he expressed his gratitude, "Thank you for sharing the notes."

As he handed her the notes, he couldn't help but notice the fear in her eyes, causing him to retreat silently without saying a word.

When Aryan left the class, the martial arts practice captivated him, and he immediately joined in. Upon arrival, he set down his belongings and entered the main area, where a few people were already practicing their skills. Without hesitation, Aryan challenged them without a second thought. One of them stepped in front of him, and before he could react, Aryan deliberately hit him and brought him down. Seeing this, a few individuals approached him from the front, but Aryan swiftly took them down with a single strike.

Seeing him intentionally provoke them, they all pounced on him simultaneously, overwhelming him to where he could no longer tolerate it. As they saw him fall to the ground, he defiantly rose again, daring them to test their abilities, and they eagerly attempted to bring him down. Despite being injured, he remains standing until the leader of the martial team approaches, at that point, Aryan launches a brutal attack, losing all sense and delivering powerful blows that leave him unfazed. More people arrived to shield the main opponent, who attempted to flee.

Aryan proceeds to ruthlessly take down everyone in his path, moving closer to his final target, who is severely injured. Aryan mercilessly attacked him, first holding his hand and then breaking it, followed by breaking his legs. Aryan relentlessly continued his assault until the person fell unconscious, resembling a lifeless body. Even though he was unconscious, Aryan shows no signs of calmness as he sits in front of him and shouts, "You used to fearlessly provide drugs in this college, but now you have nothing left. Go and inform your colleagues to meet me prior to supplying any more drugs in this campus."

Covered in blood, he confidently walks through the college, searching for a person who stands fearlessly before him. Observing her bold demeanor, he paused and remarked, "It's great to see your fearlessness return."

Without meeting his eyes, she reaches for his hand and whispers, "You're hurt. Come with me."

Divya walks in while Jahnavi is bandaging him, having witnessed Jahnavi taking care of him, and he allowed it. Aryan, completely infatuated with her, desperately tried to make eye contact, but she remained silent while tending to his wounds. Divya wants to leave, but as she turns, she notices Akanchha standing right in front of her, wanting to step in. Divya halts her but Akanchha moves her hand in a skipping motion, saying, "You don't have to keep anything from me anymore."

Akanchha approached her brother slowly, but Jahnavi intercepted her, concealing Aryan on her back, determined to shield his darker side. Akanchha reassured her, saying, "No need to hide anything from me, I already know how bad he can be. I just want to talk to my brother."

Jahnavi remains rooted in her spot, refusing to approach him, while Akanchha yelled, "You're not only disturbing the peace but also tarnishing the college's reputation. Despite our efforts to protect your career, you ultimately ruin everything for the sake of your ego. You're not my brother, who intentionally hurts others."

Jahnavi attempted to interfere, but Aryan prevented her by holding her hand. Akanchha's words hung in the air, as she said, "It's better that you leave us alone and only return when we need you the most."

Divya abruptly takes Akanchha's hand and they both leave the spot. Aryan remains silent, contemplating her harsh words, that she finally asks him to leave them alone. He appears hurt, unable to contain his emotions, and decides to leave, remembering her words.

Jahnavi stops him, her voice filled with concern, "It's not wise to confront her now; it will only make everything even worse."

In a hushed tone, he said, "Everything is finished, it's finally time to depart from college."

While taking a step forward, he appeared unsteady, prompting Jahnavi to support him, his thoughts still haunted by Akanchha's words. As Jahnavi saw him broken, she gently rested his head on her shoulder, cradling him with tenderness. "You can't simply escape this pain," she whispered, "but with time, everything heals gradually."

Aryan, no longer opposing her, tightened his grip around her, refusing to let go. Eventually, when Aryan remained motionless, she attempted to turn and face him, only to discover him unconscious.

Jahnavi, who was beside Aryan in the same room, thinking about how she watched over Akanchha. But now, she is looking after her brother. She looked into his closed eyes, feeling his pain. When she look at him, she feels a connection, but memories of seeing him with Divya make her keep her distance. As he pulled her closer, his grip on her waist tightened, expressing his longing for her affection. In response, she leaned in and placed a gentle kiss on his closed eyes, whispering, "You always claimed that my presence brought you nothing but destruction, so why do you still yearn for me to be near?"

Witnessing his deteriorating condition, she could no longer restrain herself, realizing that all of this could have been prevented if it weren't for Divya's stubbornness. Now, she is determined to bring him back at any cost and is willing to do anything for it. She remained silent, knowing everything but unable to share with anyone, her eyes filled with tears and apologizing for her helplessness. She felt Aryan's smooth kiss on her neck and held him tighter, finding solace in his care before falling asleep together.

45
Chapter Forty Five

Aryan, slowly waking up from his sleep, found Jahnavi taking care of him. When she saw he was awake, she asked, "Do you need anything?"

Aryan asked, "How exactly you bring me here?"

She answered, "I did nothing, I just did what Divya told me to do to get you out of college when you fainted. Her security team assisted us and brought us directly to this house."

Aryan stayed silent for a moment upon hearing this, then attempted to leave, but couldn't. Jahnavi questioned, "Why do you always fight with things beyond your control?"

He remains silent and then lies down, saying nothing. As she saw him resting, she prepared to leave and get something for him. Then he asked, "Why are you still here taking care of me?"

She mocks him, saying, "Because of your well-wisher who trapped us here, we can't leave until you recover."

After a while, she provided him with medication and food, but he only took the medicine and refused to eat. Seeing this, Jahnavi also noticed that he looked weak and unwell due to being on medication and not having eaten for the past 2-3 meals. Concerned, she asked him, "If you don't like my homemade dish, we can always order something instead."

Aryan attempted to get up, and she provided him with support. While walking to the kitchen, he remains stationary and requests various items before preparing something light and energizing. Jahnavi was amazed by what she learned today and he cautiously extended his hand to taste it, then immediately asked, "What is this? It tastes good."

Aryan enthusiastically explained, "This natural remedy not only heals wounds three times faster than your preferred medicine, but it also boosts immunity with no side effects."

She interrupts him, asking why he's only feeding this to her.

He responded, "I neglected to mention that it also helps relieve stress and promotes restful sleep."

Just as she was about to speak, she unexpectedly fainted in front of him. Aryan discreetly conceals the pills he blended into the soup, then gently guides her to lie down on the bed. His injured hand became trapped under her motionless body, as he struggled to free himself, he noticed she was disturbed, so he waited in silence until she woke up.

When Jahnavi gradually regained her senses, she noticed him resting beside her. She gently removed his hand from under her as she woke up. When she removed it, he asked, "Did you sleep well?"

Annoyed, she questioned, "What did you do to the soup and why am I still drowsy?"

She quickly concluded while asking him, "Did you add sleeping pills to the soup?" Upon asking this, she slowly fell asleep once more.

Aryan got off after retrieving his hand, calmly walking to the main area where he sat down. When she woke up in the evening, she angrily went to the main area to find him, only to see him reading. Noticing her awake, he discreetly conceals the document while she stands in front of him, visibly irritated, and shouts, "If you dare to do something without telling me, I will leave immediately!"

With a calm demeanor, Aryan explained, "To be able to look after me and break free from this house, it is essential that you prioritize getting enough rest."

Seeing her silent and convinced, he then walks slowly towards the kitchen side, searching for something. Soon, when he finally grasps a utensil, she swiftly takes it from him, declaring, "I no longer trust you to instruct me or tell me what you need. Just let me know, and I'll take care of it for you."

"How's Akanchha?" he asked, his voice filled with concern. "Is she feeling better or still upset with me?"

Despite her attempts to avoid it, she responded without looking, "she's fine."

Aryan then asked, "Is she still safe?"

Jahnavi held herself and responded, "Yes, Divya is there to take care of you. She knows your desires and priorities, and even before you ask, she handles everything like a guardian angel."

Aryan was just about to ask something else when she turned to his side and angrily said, "Don't ask anything else. I'm here to take care of your health, not to deliver news to you." As she was leaving, he asked from her back, "I just want to know, are you okay?"

For a moment, she ceases to listen, unsure of how to approach him afterwards. Disregarding her feelings, she departs from the main area.

At night,

Carrying dinner for her, Aryan cautiously enters her room. He finds her fast asleep and quietly exits, not wanting to disturb her slumber. In the middle of the night, Jahnavi silently made her way to the main area in search of the hidden document, but it was nowhere to be found. As she returns to her room, she pauses and gazes at the dining table, where a meal for two remains untouched by him as well.

She feels worried as he went to bed without eating. As she walks slowly to his room, she starts feeling strange. When she reaches outside his room, she loses the courage to open the door. She withdraws her hand from the door, leaves silently, and now waits for him until morning.

Aryan made his way downstairs, and when he saw her, he asked, "Did you sleep well?"

While asking this, he turns to the other side to make breakfast, only to discover it was already prepared. She gently guided him into sitting down and proceeded to serve breakfast in front of him. He took a small taste before moving the plate to her side. Upon noticing this, she asked him, "Don't you enjoy my homemade dish?"

Aryan suggested, "Because you missed last night's meal, come and enjoy this tasty food that I want to share with you."

Hearing this, she wants to apologize, but before she can say anything, he feeds her with his hand and won't stop until she finishes. Then he was heading back to his room.

When Jahnavi noticed him walking up the stairs alone, she halted him and gazed into his eyes before questioning, "Did you have trouble sleeping last night?"

As he walked in silence, Jahnavi spoke up again, concerned for his well-being. "It's not good to keep walking while you're in pain. If you want, you can rest in my room. I'll take care of things."

He stopped in his tracks, slowly, he made his way to the bed and lay down, feeling its softness beneath him. Jahnavi quietly settled herself in front of him. Upon spotting her presence, he felt a soothing sense of tranquility, eventually succumbing to a peaceful slumber. While he's resting, Jahnavi stays there for a while, taking in the peaceful surroundings.

After leaving the room, she meticulously searched every nook and cranny of the entire house, desperately seeking something important, but her efforts proved fruitless once again. Now, only one place remained unexplored - his room. She decided to give up searching and headed back to her room to attend to him.

46

Chapter Forty Six

Akanchha and Divya, who now sit in silence at the site, gaze at the assignment where Akanchha refuses to talk to anyone since that day. Divya is unaware of how to get details about Aryan while juggling her work responsibilities as the deadline for the grand event approaches. While thinking about it, she mistakenly placed the contract copy in Akanchha's files before leaving for another job.

Akanchha and Aryan have had no contact for a few days, causing tension between them and impacting Divya, who feels torn between the two. Yet, as she was about to leave to see Aryan, she suddenly halts, recollecting the night she witnessed Aryan and Jahnavi growing closer. This instills fear in her, as she contemplates the possibility of moving in and facing the same circumstances. The mere thought of it compels her to ruthlessly discard her belongings, unable to tolerate the idea of someone else caring for him instead of her.

She appears increasingly desperate to meet Aryan, but then restrains herself, considering that if she doesn't go to that place, she won't have to witness anything worse. This thought brings her a sense of calm, as she has yet to witness anything, and it was merely her speculation. After deciding, she hesitantly returns to work and calls the doctor to check on Aryan immediately. Now, she anxiously awaits his health report.

Akanchha, sitting alone at home, discovers a new document in her files. She takes it and begins reading it, and after finishing, she reads it again multiple times before adding more details and keeping it secure. Divya, who finally received his health report, discovered that his wounds will heal in just a few more days. Now, she waits patiently.

Aryan, who has made a remarkable recovery and regained his ability to walk effortlessly, is still facing obstacles when attempting strenuous tasks. One night, he abruptly woke up from his sleep and discovered that Jahnavi was nowhere to be found. He appears concerned for her and leaves his bed to search for her. As he made his way into the main room, he noticed her sitting in his chair and going through his things. He gently removed his belongings from her hand and, at the same time, held her hand, saying, "It's late. You should rest."

He brings her back to the room and has her lie on the bed. He sits at the front while she falls asleep slowly, but Aryan remains awake and keeps looking at her all night.

When Jahnavi wakes up, she is surprised to find him sleeping next to her. This is the first time he has come so close to her, and she is unsure how to react to these new feelings. She now knows how to help him sleep peacefully, something he used to miss out on every day. Aryan appears to be doing well and his report indicates a faster recovery. When she learns this, she feels down, unsure of the feeling. It's not love, nor does she like him, but the thought of leaving him makes her worried, as if she's losing something.

She continued walking while deep in thought, until she finally arrived at the last room, which was always locked. Spotting this, her excitement grew as she anticipated discovering something important inside. Not finding him nearby, she unlocked the door leading to complete darkness. She attempts to brighten the room, but fails. Then, she switches on her flashlight and searches for the socket. There, she discovers a specific wiring and accidentally turns on the switch, illuminating the room. She stands in the center of the newly lit circle.

She appeared amazed and proceeded to uncover the covered items one by one and at last she found a piano. While uncovering it, she discovers a few of his unfinished compositions. Taking a seat, she hesitantly begins reading them, slowly connecting with Aryan's emotions and empathizing with his pain. While reading, she starts developing feelings for him but stops when she comes across the word "well-wisher."

She becomes so consumed by deciphering his emotions that she almost forgets everything that happened in the past, only to have her own precious feelings taken away by herself. At this moment, a tear rolled down her cheek as she tried to read which was only meant for his well-wisher. She watched helplessly as her precious feelings slowly faded away, desperately trying to recover them. But when they were completely gone, she was left empty-handed. In a fit of rage, she mercilessly threw and broke everything in the room, attempting to destroy anything that held her feelings.

47
Chapter Forty Seven

Despite everything being destroyed, she still can't find peace and tears up the note that expressed his feelings. Seeking to leave, she unintentionally injures herself on broken objects, resulting in her losing balance. Aryan, witnessing this, holds her tightly and focuses solely on her tearful eyes, which reflect her pain and desire to avoid facing him, as she tries to depart. Holding her hand, he lifts her into his arms, rescuing her from the room that continues to hurt her. He placed her on the bed and gently removed the stuck piece from her foot, then bandaged it and attended to her needs. Without making eye contact, she told him, "Please go away. I don't need your concern or your presence. Just leave me alone."

Aryan quietly placed the medicine and first aid box next to her before leaving the room. Jahnavi, feeling lost and hurt, searches for her patience, finding solace next to him as she clutches the sheets, covered in tears, longing to release her pain, still able to feel Aryan's warmth in the wrapped sheet. She falls asleep, still feeling his care even in his absence.

Sitting in the main room, Aryan's thoughts are solely focused on her pain and the memories that bring tears to her eyes. He lost his patience while thinking this, but all he could do was wait for her to recover. Divya, feeling lost without Aryan, couldn't resist reading his diary to relive his feelings for her and express her own sense of helplessness without him. Slowly, she begins playing the piano, reminding herself of the notes Aryan left. She played for a while, fully immersed in her emotions, convinced he was there. As she opened her eyes and didn't see him, her frustration returned and she stopped playing. Even this couldn't replace the void that only his presence could fill.

Divya was sitting helplessly when Akanchha appeared and returned the incomplete document that she had left in her file. She slowly examines the document that has been modified. As she read the concluding lines of the composition, her excitement grew and she eagerly asked, "How did you manage to do it?"

Akanchha responded, "While I may not be as clever as him, I still understand my brother's emotions and can relate to them because we share the same blood. Let's see if my insight can be of any assistance."

Divya sensed that Akanchha was feeling uneasy and realized they were going through the same thing. She gently took her hand and invited her to sit beside her, saying, "If you're hurting, why be alone? Let's make this feeling even more valuable."

She begins playing the melody, following the modified notes Akanchha added to her brother's composition, and they both fall into a contemplative silence, grasping its true significance.

48

Chapter Forty Eight

Jahnavi hasn't left her room for nearly 2 days. Aryan, feeling impatient, goes to check on her and finds her health deteriorated and still unconscious. He searches for supplements and medicine, taking everything, then holds her in his arms. He makes her drink water first, followed by a small portion of liquid diet. After waiting for a while, he finally gives her medicine, which she takes while feeling dizzy.

Aryan prepare everything at night, then sneak into her room to check if she was awake. Seeing her resting, he sat near her feet and slowly remove the bandage. Despite feeling pain, she keeps her eyes closed as he tightly holds her feet to finish dressing, causing her discomfort. Once it was finished, Aryan left, leaving behind Jahnavi who remained stubborn. After some time, she was lifted effortlessly and found herself back in his arms, despite her reluctance to face him.

"Allow me to handle what needs to be done, and once you're healed, you can go freely. No one will impede you, but until then, let me take care of you."

As she listens, her resistance fades, and he begins to feed her slowly. Once she finishes eating, he silently departs, while she, with closed eyes, murmurs softly, "I am afraid of being alone in silence for too long."

Aryan listened and slowly sat down beside her, positioning himself so she wouldn't have to face him, as she had wanted. Aryan, who had been watching over her, sensed something strange as dawn approached. Without glancing to her side, he cautiously reached out to touch her cold hand, only to have her suddenly grip his hand tightly. While asleep, she pulls him closer, savoring his warmth as she holds him tightly. He appears slightly insecure, as he wishes to avoid further offending her. Gradually, he holds her tightly, as she finally finds her patience and appears calm. Aryan, who has been feeling insecure until now, focuses only on her well-being when she asks for his care, and now he rests with her.

Despite it being late in the morning, Aryan, still asleep, embraces her even more tightly as he senses her longing for his care. Jahnavi, feeling close to him, hesitantly kissed his chest, confirming he was still here watching over her and it wasn't a dream. As evening approached, Aryan woke up from a restful sleep and realized Jahnavi was not in bed.

Upon seeing this, he immediately jumps out of bed and rushes to the main area, where he notices Jahnavi walking in pain towards the door. Aryan remains silent and eagerly awaits her decision. Standing at the door, Jahnavi hesitates, grabs the handle, and suddenly asks, "You don't want to stop me, do you?"

Aryan walked slowly towards her, intending to open the door for her. She grabbed his hand and turned towards him, realizing there was so much she needed to say. Aryan's words cut through the silence, "You had every opportunity to leave, yet the unlocked door held no appeal. It's because you've seen me shattered that you refuse to go."

As he carefully locked the gate, he spoke with determination, "I understand that learning about my past might be painful for you, but I'm ready to do whatever it takes to change."

Slowly, he raised his hand towards her, hoping for her to come back. But Jahnavi, upon hearing his words, couldn't believe him. Despite feeling hurt, she stood her ground and looked into his eyes as she said, "I have to go because nothing can be changed now."

When he looked into her eyes, he could sense her true emotions. He felt hopeful, but her rejection didn't align with her desires. However, he withdrew his hand and said, "I won't prevent you, but I'd like you to stay for dinner before you go."

She could sense his reluctance to let her go and tried to refuse, but ultimately gave in and agreed to leave at midnight.

He gradually approached her as she pressed herself against the door, his gaze starting at her eyes and slowly moving downward. He observed how she carried herself, noticing his admiration for her, but then he looked away from her feet, which caused her pain even while standing. In response, he gently embraced her and guided her back to the room.

He enters the room and instructs her to sit calmly before retrieving a package from the wardrobe, which he gives to her, saying, "I want you to be prepared for dinner," and then he leaves.

49

Chapter Forty Nine

Jahnavi sets the package aside and ponders whether opening it will have any impact on him. With a mind full of thoughts, she struggled to decide what to do, and hours passed while she continued to ponder. Aryan knocked at the door and waited, but when there was no reply, Aryan opened the door. He entered the room and saw her, dressed in the well-wishing dress he had gifted her for dinner. Speechless, he observed her attempting to tie the knot of her heels while hindered by bandages.

Aryan, who is running late for dinner, approaches her and takes off her heels, saying, "You no longer need these."

Without hesitation, he held her tightly and led her straight to the dining room, where she found that nothing had been prepared except for a covered plate. She glanced at him where he subtly tilted so she could inspect the concealed dish. When she uncovered it, she discovered a small assortment of handmade cookies. Taking one, he signaled for her to taste it. As she savors it, her eyes show enchantment, indicating her enjoyment, prompting him to move to the next spot briefly, before continuing forward.

Aryan takes her to explore every corner of the house, revealing various gifts in each place, all while holding her in his arms. By doing this for her, he was giving her new memories that, though small and simple, were precious to her. In addition, she was experiencing a new version of him that she had never witnessed until now. He was making an effort to create and share a joyful moment that was solely dedicated to her.

Her mood and feelings towards him gradually shifted as she found herself smiling, cheering him on, and becoming an active participant in these precious, intimate moments they shared. With each step he took towards his room, he could feel her clutching onto him, her grip on his shoulder and collar becoming firmer, as if she wanted to block out the memory of the moment when she went alone in that room.

"Keep your gaze fixed on me," Aryan urged, assuring her, "By the time you leave today, your mind will be filled with nothing but joyful memories."

While she listens, she gradually opens her eyes and then opens the door slowly, where he enters with her. He guided her to sit on the bed and then moved a few steps back, taking a seat a little distance away. She watched him closely, curious about his actions. When he saw her fully attentive, he pulled out a piece of paper and started writing, never breaking eye contact. Jahnavi, meeting his gaze, was able to grasp all of his emotions that he had expressed in writing.

For a few hours, they remained fixated on each other, and once he finished, he carried that sentiment with him as he approached her, enveloping her in an embrace before heading towards the window with a view of the lake. Observing the beauty of nature, she appeared blessed. When she looked into his eyes, she sensed he was patiently waiting to reveal something to her. Then, she left the room. Before departing, Jahnavi took a slow glance at the room, where they had spent several hours in silence.

Despite the silence, she managed to express everything she wanted to, and now she carries a sweet memory of this room as she leaves. She turned her head slowly towards him and asked, "Where are you taking me?"

"I've got one more spot to show you," said Aryan.

As he walks towards the last room, she suddenly recalls the mess she made there. Despite her warning, he insists on entering the room to share a special moment with her.

He persisted in opening the door in the pitch-black room until he arrived at the very spot where she had retrieved the tiny remote from his front pocket. When she turns on the switch, the room lights up, creating a pleasant ambiance. As she slowly looked around, she noticed that the light he used was adjusting itself and all the messy items had been replaced with beautiful flowers and antiques. As she looked at it, he continued walking towards their final destination - a candlelight dinner that awaited them.

With a gentle motion, he guided her to her seat, revealing the elaborate feast he had meticulously prepared for her. Without diverting his gaze, he began feeding her each dish in succession. Whenever he acts this way, she feels as though he is divulging his wishes to someone dear, while Jahnavi remains tight-lipped about his actions and treatment. Now, all she cared about was his changed behavior towards her, something she had never felt before. And when she had finished everything, Aryan finally presented the last gift he had made from his emotions. He took out the paper he had written for her and gave it to her. She took it from his hand and glanced at his calm demeanor, prepared to express his feelings for her. Just as she was about to open the note, she abruptly halted, lost in thought.

Without speaking, Jahnavi got up and walked over to his side, not stopping when she reached him. She continued on, passing through the room until she reached a little corner where she revealed the piano. She faces him, extending her hand towards his side, observing his reaction. Aryan hesitates to ask her, but notices her lingering anticipation. As he looked into her eyes, pleading for him to trust her this time, he began to walk towards her.

As he arrives, he gently takes her hand and, seeing his trust in her, she guides him to sit. She stepped back a few paces to observe him as he sat at his music table, admiring his appearance for a moment. Finally, she spoke, "The night isn't over yet, and before I go, I want you to give me your words as a gift."

She hands the unread note back to him and says, "I don't want paper, I want to experience your feelings for me. If you won't share that with me, I don't want your gifts. I care about your emotions and don't want them to be hurt when I'm near you."

As he listened, he glanced into her eyes and saw her desperate curiosity. Upon witnessing his silence, she finally handed his note back, declaring, "I have received the answer to all my questions."

Just as she was about to leave empty-handed, she abruptly stops near the door and turns towards Aryan, who daringly plays the notes but cannot continue. Jahnavi, who sensed his pain, could feel it all as she witnessed his hesitation. Aryan sought support from her, as he couldn't handle it alone, and she didn't want to leave.

Noticing his condition, she discreetly signaled him to focus only on her and ignore everything else. Aryan attempted to play a tune as she slowly walked towards him. Jahnavi patiently waits for him to reveal everything, standing near the spot where she took each step and he played the tune accordingly. Aryan's emotions come pouring out as he remembers her tear-filled eyes while singing for her.

Aryan, while singing the final line of his composition, approaches her. Her eyes are filled with tears, which he gently wipes away before handing her the note. "This feeling is exclusively yours, and no one, including me, can take it away from you."

Jahnavi, standing in her spot, is left speechless as she truly comprehends the significance of Aryan's gift, which ultimately erases the last remnants of her worst memories. While taking the note, she hugged him tightly. She was crying, feeling an overwhelming sense of preciousness she had never experienced before. Aryan cautiously explored her body, causing her to embrace him more tightly as he held her with gentleness.

Stepping onto his feet, she lowers herself to his level and gazes into his eyes, where, Aryan said, "I promised to make changes, and now your presence no longer brings me pain."

She responded, "My name is Miss Trouble, remember?"

As he listens, he smiles and recalls the name he gave her, then gently kisses her forehead, expressing, "thankyou for your support in helping me overcome my painful past."

Upon hearing this, Jahnavi immediately suppresses her emotions and gazes directly into his eyes, saying, "It's midnight, I should go now."

Aryan, who had finally found peace with her, became quiet and helpless when he heard this, realizing there was nothing more he could do to make her stay. Jahnavi, noticing his silence, reluctantly prepares to leave but not before softly kissing his neck and murmuring, "It was a wonderful evening."

Aryan closes his eyes, unable to watch her leave, feeling her care for the last time. Jahnavi departs from the room, leaving Aryan, who chooses not to speak and allows her to leave without resistance. She walked to the main door, looking back to capture the fading moments she had just experienced. Unable to do anything, she watched helplessly until she could no longer contain herself, and left the house with tear-filled eyes.

50

Chapter Fifty

Aryan's sense of calm evaporated as he inspected the arrangements he had put together for her, realizing they were all in vain. Annoyance welled up inside him as he surveyed the scene, and just as his anger threatened to consume him, the doorbell chimed unexpectedly. As he listens, he walks desperately to the side of the door and immediately opens it, revealing her long-awaited return to this house and to him.

She was standing a bit away from him moved forward and entered the house. When she stepped in, Aryan seemed even more desperate while looking at her. With one hand, he angrily grabs her hand and tightly holds her hair while passionately kissing her neck and body. When he does that, she loved it completely. She silently accepts his treatment, allowing him to vent his anger on her. Aryan, being rude at first, gradually kisses her, starting from her lips and reaching all the way to her heart, noticing how her lips crave his affection.

He angrily stepped away from her and said, "Right now, I'm not myself, so please leave me alone."

"I was once fearful, but now I am determined to care for your wounds that I have overlooked," she replied.

Smoothly, she grips his hand, causing it to constrict around her neck, and whispers, "Don't be kind to me, unleash all your anger on me, it's what I desire most."

Aryan remains silent as he slowly removes his hand from her neck and gently guides it down to her waist, before finally embracing her and leading her to the room. He laid her on the bed and removed his shirt, then joined her on the bed to gently undress her upper body. With admiration, he gently touches her body, savoring the moment, before embracing her tightly and indulging in passionate kisses and intense bites. When he treats her rudely, he feels a sensation that intensifies the pain he inflicts, leading him to crave her love desperately.

He openly expresses his anger towards her for abandoning him. In an instant, she pushes him away, takes control, and glances at his side where he appears angry and desperate for her. She noticed his restlessness and decided to administer a stronger drug, feeding it to him while she patiently awaits its effects. Within moments, it started functioning, causing her to appear calm as she now had full control over his senses, allowing her to treat him as she desired.

She steps away from him, just out of reach, where he can see her but not fully have her. As she does this, she begins to touch herself, causing pain while gripping herself tightly. There she is, sensually biting and kissing herself, driving him to the brink of desperation, while slowly undressing. She climbs into bed and begins to slowly explore his naked body, starting with removing his jeans. She passionately kisses him, her pain transforming into desire, biting his lip before moving to his neck, alternating between gentle licks and bites, all the while her fingers entwined in his hair.

Her care for him has heightened his desires to the point where he finally confessed, "I need you."

When he utters the same word, he recalls a glimpse of that dark night, causing him to pause until he can remember the girl, she kisses his lips, slowly captivating him.

Aryan, fully engrossed in her, carefully undressed her from the waist down. She pulls him closer, fueling his wild desire as they passionately make love, expressing both anger and desperation solely for her. He mistreats her, gradually turning her into his slave to fulfill his desires, and she accepts it all, giving herself completely.

As they lay in bed together, he gradually relaxes while she climbs on top of him, gazing into his eyes, craving more of his love.

Witnessing her longing, he relentlessly provided the love she yearned for, until she climaxed twice. She slowly came to rest, but his desire remained unfulfilled as he continued to ask for more love. Seeing this, she got back on top of him, looking into his eyes where she could sense his desperation for her. While making love, she brings him both pleasure and pain, just as he does to her, leaving Aryan completely captivated and craving more until the break of dawn when they finally find rest.

Divya, lying beside him, gazed into his eyes and then his lips, still yearning for his affection. She no longer wants to rest because being away from him for so long, and now she seeks his warmth by hiding herself in his arms, kissing him gently near his heart, and when she does, he feels a sensation and holds her even tighter. Despite her ongoing attempts to eradicate the darkness, he remains fearful of doing so, yet finds solace in her ability to attend to his every need.

51

Chapter Fifty One

Aryan woke up late in the morning feeling dizzy. He found himself half naked and noticed Divya partially undressed. His heart was drawn to her, and he noticed marks on her body. He gently held her hand. Then, Divya took the sheet and carefully covered both of them. Under the sheets, she yearned for his closeness, finding solace in Aryan's gentle touch.

Despite feeling dizzy, Aryan realizes that she isn't hurting by his touch. She quickly covers his eyes to prevent him from seeing her bruises, then gently kisses his heart to soothe his senses. Slowly, she moves her hair aside from around her neck and holds his hair from the back, causing him to stick his tongue to her neck. There, he kisses her gently, giving her a sweet sensation. She holds him tighter, eagerly desiring more. He noticed her desire and responded by pressing his lips harder against hers, sensually biting. As he intensified, she craved even more of his affection.

Aryan, who was fulfilling his desire, appears to be falling back into her care, which Divya intentionally orchestrated to make him rest again. Aryan felt dizzy and eventually fell asleep, only to wake up in the evening and realize he was alone. All night he sits silently, pondering as he holds the new document, where he finally discovers that both girls came for a specific purpose.

Akanchha, seated in one spot, was engrossed in her work, lost in her thoughts. Suddenly, she unveils the concealed previous work and studies a picture capturing Divya and Aryan's apparent intimacy. In a separate photo with Jahnavi, she notices Aryan behaving intimately. She had one picture in hand and needed to uplift the project by shooting the missing one again, so she looked at her phone to call him.

Akanchha observed visitors who went straight to the CEO cabin upon entering the site. Upon hearing harsh voices coming from the cabin, everyone ceased working. Upon witnessing this, Akanchha hesitantly approached the cabin and found that they were demanding the incomplete work, leaving Divya at a loss for words. Upon noticing Akanchha, she discreetly gestured not to interrupt, but Jahnavi abruptly approached and requested additional time. However, they disregarded her pleas and continued yelling at them.

They finally called out the name Aryan and accused him of being a defaulter. Divya seemed impatient and asked them to leave while speaking harshly to them. Akanchha intervened when she saw the situation turning against her, prompting Divya to ask her to leave. However, Akanchha greeted them and introduced herself.

Everyone seems interested in her after finding out she's related to Aryan, and they asked her directly to sign the charges on behalf of his brother. Divya found herself backed into a corner by Aryan's actions, causing Akanchha to step forward and willingly shoulder all the blame. Jahnavi's voice filled with concern as she warned, "This is not right. What if your brother finds out? He could cause even more destruction if he realizes you're in danger again."

Akanchha answered, "He's not present, and I don't see anyone else willing to take the fall for him. I will sign the contract because we care about him and it's the only way to ensure he completes the work on time. And remember, don't contact him this time or everything will go downhill."

Both girls were silent while the studio partners instructed to draft a new contract, and eventually Akanchha signed it. Divya and Jahnavi also signed the contract since she was a minor, making the contract potentially void. As they all signed the contract, Akanchha was about to hand it to the studio manager when a hand suddenly appeared. The person who appeared at the spot was Aryan, which left everyone in shock.

Holding the contract tightly, he confronted them, his voice filled with anger. "I see you made a deal without informing me, but I never gave my consent to it. We need to set up a new deal, so until then, all of you can go."

He was taking the contract with himself, and they all voiced their disapproval, saying, "This is not how we conduct business. We both agreed to the terms of the contract, and now you're violating it, which is completely unjust."

Aryan angrily shouted, "Don't lecture me about business ethics. You've already made a major mistake by making a new deal without informing me, and I just received an email about it half an hour ago. Yet, I'm still speaking to you calmly.

Aryan noticed a security guard approaching, he swiftly took him down, causing a terrified reaction from everyone witnessing the incident. The main manger was about to threaten him, and in that moment, Aryan firmly grasped his coat collar, asserting, "Don't underestimate me. I won't be defeated in any scenario. Maybe you have lots of money, but I have powerful resources that make me untouchable." Without asking anything further, they all left.

Aryan, who held the new contract, appeared visibly annoyed as he tore it up immediately. Then, he glanced at Divya and Jahnavi and cautioned them, "I am giving you all one final warning to not make any more commitments without consulting me, otherwise, I will hold you accountable for the consequences, not myself."

As everyone remained silent, he said, "I need this site relocated to the college right away."

Divya instructed everyone to prepare for the move and was about to leave, when Akanchha asked Jahnavi from behind, "You called him despite my request not to involve him."

Divya glances in the direction where she noticed Akanchha interrogating Jahnavi, who performs this in secrecy. Divya appeared shocked upon learning this, while Jahnavi calmly responded to Akanchha, "He's the one who told me not to involve you in any matters, and when you refuse to listen, I have no choice but to finally call him."

Upon hearing this, Akanchha seems annoyed and abruptly departs. Divya was leaving, and Jahnavi, holding her hand, asked, "Did you purposely call them and do everything?"

Divya replied, stating, "I do whatever feels right, and you, my dear, have yet to give me everything he gave you."

Jahnavi seem shocked but when she thinks about her present, she then took a stand for her thing for the first time which she doesn't want to give it to her and said, "I already gave you every detail you requested, and as a result, you were able to easily enter the house once I left him incomplete."

Divya gets closer, softly touching her body, and says, "You admitted that you received his care and sensational touch, which also belongs to me. Until you return everything I sent you there, I won't stop. It's best if both siblings follow my instructions, I don't know how you'll do it, but make it happen since I've already taken the first step."

52

Chapter Fifty Two

Jahnavi and Akanchha haven't spoken to each other in a few days. Jahnavi attempted to speak to her, but Akanchha interrupted angrily, "Why do you even bother caring about him when he clearly doesn't value your support? And this time, when he appeared, something even more dreadful occurred."

Listening to the harsh words about Aryan, Jahnavi immediately interrupts, "Everyone always sees his worst side, but you are blood related to him. Why can't you see his pain? Like everyone else, you can't comprehend your brother's true nature. Despite saving everyone, all he gets is hatred, and even his sister doesn't believe in him. In the end, you effortlessly asked him to go away—how heartless you can be! He does all of this because he cares for us and acts like a true brother when any of us are in trouble. If this is what a true brother is, then I am envious of you for having the most caring brother anyone could ever have."

With that, she departs and leaves Akanchha to ponder her words. Divya, who was impatient, called Jahnavi and gave her a one-week deadline to execute the first part of their plan.

Jahnavi, unable to find a solution to make the siblings cooperate, finally retreated to the rehearsal room. Playing the melody softly, she began practicing alone to find peace. Eventually, another person joins her and they dance together, assisting Jahnavi with the same steps. When their eyes met, she whispered, "This melody captivates me."

Jahnavi answered, "This is your brother's composition."

Akanchha suddenly stopped dancing, appearing shocked. Jahnavi holds Akanchha's hand and invites her to dance again, leaving Akanchha unsure of how to react. Jahnavi comforts her by saying, "There are many reasons and situations that can break your heart. During those times, our family, friends, and trusted individuals provide us with hope and strength. In your situation, you have me, Divya, and your brother around you. We will always take care of you, so there's no need to apologize or feel sorry. As your friend and elder sister, I promise to always take care of you, just like your brother wanted."

Akanchha holds her hand and assures her, "I promise to keep your promise safe."

In a surprising turn of events, Jahnavi somehow regained her friend. While working one day, Akanchha casually asked her if she knew why he erased all the data, leaving only specific photos of Divya and Aryan.

Upon hearing this, she is reminded of the past once more and becomes visibly unsettled. Unable to concentrate any longer, she abruptly requests to depart. Akanchha was fully engrossed in her work, while Jahnavi accidentally left her phone behind before leaving, and later Akanchha also left, locking the room. The next day, when Jahnavi returned, she searched everywhere for her missing phone but couldn't find it, even with the help of the college staff. Finally, she was departing, where she witnessed everyone gathering in the central area.

While glancing at the screen displaying upcoming songs, she halted abruptly upon hearing a familiar melody in the midst of the crowd. As she turned around, she caught a glimpse of the newly released music video streaming through studio partners. As she listened to the new composition, composed exclusively for her by Aryan, she couldn't help but feel a rush of emotions. Everyone seemed amazed, their eyes wide as they listened to Aryan's new composition, while she stood there in shock.

Observing the scene, it was clear that everyone saw her and Aryan as an unbeatable couple with perfect chemistry in the music video. After a while, everyone started moving aside when they saw Aryan coming, where she last saw Akanchha present. Aryan watching the video doesn't know how it was released, as he didn't share it with anyone. While he was pondering this, a college staff member suddenly appeared, delivering an unidentified package in his name.

Upon opening the package, he discovered a phone that had been delivered to him. As he opened it, he realized it was Jahnavi's phone. Before he could ask anything, the studio partners arrived with his staff, who stood calmly in front of him. He recalled the previous encounter when he had pressured everyone, but in the end, he released the song under his own studio name. Aryan, upon seeing him, had one question: "How did you come across this composition and where did it come from?"

He silently displayed the mail to him. After viewing the details, he unlocked the phone and checked the sent mail. He comes across the attachment that was sent from Jahnavi's phone. Witnessing his silence and apparent confusion while learning, everyone grew terrified.

Slowly making her way forward, Akanchha walks towards her brother. With Jahnavi's involvement evident, the studio manager announced in front of everyone, "Now that we're all here, let's sign the contract. Aryan Mishra has willingly released his new track with our studio. He has already committed to delivering three compositions, one of which has been delivered today."

Aryan remains silent while he continued, "It's late, but we don't want to take any action. We want to see his new composition before deciding on the remaining part. But before we go, we want him to grant us the rights to this composition."

Akanchha handed the pen to his brother and said, "Sign this contract to avoid more disputes."

Aryan saw hope in his sister's eyes, despite her fear that things could go wrong. He believed her request could restore trust like before. Aryan took the pen without a word and signed the contract, surrendering all his rights to the studio. Once he hands the contract to the manager, everyone praises and blesses him for doing the right thing. The studio manager and his team left.

Aryan continued to receive praise from everyone for his actions. Akanchha becomes emotional upon receiving everyone's appraisal, and she glances at her brother who silently agrees with her. Before she can say anything, Jahnavi arrives. Aryan hands her phone back and refuses to let go, saying he never expected such a gift from her, but now they are even because he repaid her for her kindness to his sister. Thank you for finally sharing what hurts you the most - my care for you, which you ended on a positive note. However, I want you to be happy after this.

He returns her phone before silently departing. Akanchha finally embraces Jahnavi, expressing gratitude for revealing a side of her brother that she herself was unaware of, regardless of the potential consequences.

Jahnavi replied, "As long as we have you, he won't lose his sanity, as he had already demonstrated in front of everyone. So, I expect you to apologize for everything you've done in the past."

Agreeing, Akanchha expresses, "I need your help in this matter as well, similar to how you helped me this time."

While thinking about the misunderstanding, Jahnavi's gentle grip held her back, offering comfort and reassurance. Aryan's trust in her is shattered after accepting her as the culprit, leaving her feeling low; she clings tightly to Akanchha to find solace.

53

Chapter Fifty Three

Divya, who had been absent for several days despite the significant events at the college, finally comes back. She returned after receiving news from the studio partners and began searching for Aryan. Eventually, she found him standing in front of the library, hesitating to enter the room. Upon observing this, she came to the realization that he is not okay and now seeks the return of his possessions. She noticed him desperately wanting his diary, so she considered handing it over but stopped abruptly when she saw a poster of Aryan and Jahnavi appearing close in their new album release. She withholds it from him for now, as there's something else she needs to attend to.

Akanchha and the rest of the staff who participated in the campaign were summoned immediately for the meeting. Divya, who initially displayed the new music album poster, questioned, "Who published this without seeking approval from higher authorities?"

Divya noticed that everyone was silent and when no one spoke up, she pointed out the name under the poster - Akanchha Mishra. Akanchha came forward, her silence speaking volumes. Divya questioned her, reminding her of the protocol established at the beginning of the campaign. "Did you discuss anything with either of us, as we had agreed?"

Divya understood the answer from the silence in her words, causing her to angrily throw things and yell at the entire crew, particularly Akanchha who remained silent. Jahnavi eventually arrives. Divya lost her patience when she saw her, and ended up yelling at her and eventually told Akanchha that she was no longer part of the program because she didn't want anyone who disobeyed her.

When Jahnavi took a stand for Akanchha, Divya asked her to leave the project too. Upon hearing this, Akanchha prevents Jahnavi from interfering and agrees to leave the project independently, silently departing the meeting.

Akanchha packed her belongings and was ready to leave the college. Before departing, she noticed Jahnavi standing behind her, who had tried everything she could for her, even though she couldn't do much. Akanchha expresses her heartfelt gratitude to her. Upon her departure, she made a point not to look back and eventually shut her eyes. Upon encountering the person in front of her, she silently wrapped her arms around him, tears welling in her eyes, leaving him stunned.

He restrains her until she calms down after some time when she regains awareness. She grabbed her camera and all project-related files, handing them over as she admitted, "You were right all along. I shouldn't have continued working; I should have focused on my studies. I've decided to quit my project and prioritize my studies. Once this is over, you won't have any more problems because I trust you to ensure that your presence doesn't harm anyone, which is what matters most to me.

Finally, my work is complete and I am peacefully departing from this college. With a smile on her face, she hands all the stuff to her brother and silently leaves the campus.

Aryan stood in silence, holding the stuff and observing her unfinished work that she never abandoned like this. Finally, he looks in the direction where Jahnavi texted him to meet. Wondering why she called him urgently, he noticed that she didn't seem well and wanted to know what was wrong. Spotting him approaching, she quickly departs before he can reach her. Noticing both girls leaving without saying anything, he becomes suspicious.

Without delay, Divya stops all connections and motion occurring behind her. She appears to be fine now as she moves away from the spot where Aryan remains seated, calmly observing the beauty of nature, refraining from dwelling on the details, but contemplating Akanchha's abrupt resignation. Slowly, he reached for her file and started inspecting the details, delving into her unfinished project with a preplanned strategy. As he moved forward, he eventually spotted the first poster of his newly released album.

When he looked at it, he noticed that his sister's name was listed as the lead photographer. This surprised him because he knew that Jahnavi had taken the picture. So why was Akanchha's name mentioned? Recalling this, he realizes that his album was released by Jahnavi and both tasks were done covertly. Discovering her intentional actions, he crushed the poster in annoyance, realizing it was a trap for both of them. Now he is worried, wondering why she did all of this. After much contemplation, he finally departs the campus late at night.

54

Chapter Fifty Four

On the next day,

When everyone came back to college, they were amazed by the theme that Aryan had prepared and was still working on. Once he finished, he left to gather the remaining decoration items. Upon returning, he discovered the spot had been destroyed. Observing which Aryan remain patient and resume constructing the spot. He spent the whole day on the college campus, working day and night. This time, he prepared an even more beautiful spot and now he waits.

At dawn, a group of thugs and hooligans entered the campus and proceeded to search for something. They utilize a tracker to reach the destination, and once inside the room, Aryan cunningly locks everyone in and gradually releases a toxic gas that renders them unconscious. Upon doing so, he proceeded to enter the room and began tying everyone up with a rope. However, one person seemed to be awake and managed to escape the trap. Upon observing him running, Aryan permitted him to flee without difficulty and then get back to the spot.

Upon their return to college, everyone noticed that Aryan had set up the next spot even more beautifully than before. Everyone started taking pictures of the spot as he walked slowly towards the student and calmly requested his camera. As he takes their picture, a crowd gathers and asks to be photographed with his theme.

Aryan's calm and friendly nature makes everyone feel good as all the college students gather at the main ground to enjoy the shoot.

His changed behavior left everyone in disbelief, as they watched him create new themes at dawn, only to witness him systematically destroy them each night, before starting anew the next day. Observing him, Jahnavi decided to walk over to the spot while he was preoccupied with capturing the shot. He carefully stores all the pictures he took in his sister's file, capturing various faces with different emotions, all tied together by an everlasting theme. Her amazement was evident as she observed his work, particularly Akanchha's camera, which piqued her curiosity to examine the stored files, prompting her to take the camera.

When she finally opened it, she came across old pictures of Aryan and herself that had been stored on the camera chip. Aryan was the one who kept the picture safe without giving it to anyone. She appears emotional as she recalls their final day at his house. Aryan noticed some attractive girls and started taking their pictures without permission, while Jahnavi silently took the chip and left the spot. Instead of opposing him, they wanted to take a picture with the real model, Aryan.

He took several pictures with different girls, but ended up getting stuck with one and is now doing a serious photoshoot with her. Out of nowhere, a confident stud strides towards him from the crowd, accusing, "Hey, she's mine and you're getting too handsy with her."

Aryan replied, "Watch your words when talking about her as 'your girl'. Let me make it clear this time, she's your sister now. If anyone tries to destroy this pure bond, I will personally intervene, and I assure you, neither of us wants that to occur."

He reluctantly passes the camera to him, resigning himself to the only option left, and begins taking pictures of them. Aryan gradually moves closer during the shoot, but suddenly sees nothing and continues to get closer and closer to her. Finally, in anger, the boy throws the camera. Aryan's attention shifted to his trembling left hand, and he remained silent, clutching his girl until he departed. As soon as he left, he quickly pushed the girl away and walked towards the camera. Upon noticing the broken lens, he hurriedly went to the track recording room, where he kept all his work secure.

Upon arrival, he grabbed his sister's camera and attempted to replace the broken lens, but it didn't function. Frustrated by the failure, he grows impatient and heads towards the college's other section where the campaign work is stored securely. Once he arrives, he desperately searches for the lens, attempting to fix each one individually with no success. Frustrated by his unsuccessful attempts, he becomes annoyed and angrily throws the things. A person behind him handed him the lens, remarking, "When anger consumes you, even the clearest things become blurry, even when they're right in front of your eyes."

Disregarding what she said, he quickly grabbed the lens and managed to adjust it successfully. Now that it was working, he eagerly wanted to see the picture he had taken. Seeing all the pictures safe and intact in the chip made him appear calm. Finally, he turned to thank her but found no one there, realizing it was only him. Not seeing anyone around, he locked the room and left.

As he reached his shooting spot, he abruptly halted, sensing something suspicious. When he attempted to move forward again, he detected the smell of kerosene oil. Just as he was about to think, the decorated spot suddenly caught fire, leaving him shocked as he watched all the preparations turn to ashes. Aryan, who remained motionless, held the camera and kept all the details within it secure. When he eventually recalls Akanchha's camera left in the burning spot, he frantically rushes towards the fire. Despite everyone's attempts to prevent him, he paid no heed and ultimately security and staff had to step in, but he overpowered them and entered the burning area. The rescue team's staff attempts to extinguish the fire where Aryan has been trapped for a while. Once they manage to control the fire, they prepare to enter and rescue Aryan.

As they were about to enter, they witnessed Aryan emerging from the burning area in a terrible condition, somehow managing to walk. Despite being engulfed in intense flames, he struggled to breathe and felt his body burning. Despite his dire condition, he managed to glance at the camera and found it empty. Seeing this, he yelled in annoyance, feeling the unbearable pain of being exposed to the open environment. They poured water over his body to soothe his burning pain.

He finally lost consciousness due to his breathing problem. The rescue team transport him to the hospital. Everyone appeared shocked and concerned for Aryan, who tried to protect his work containing precious memories of his college experience, which he embraced openly for the first time. Divya, who was at the hospital, became impatient and angry when she saw Aryan's deteriorating health. She immediately called her men, saying, "I want that bastard who did this. Take him down by any means necessary."

It took nearly 48 hours to recover from the heat stroke, which resulted in damage to his breathing and nerves. Aryan abruptly woke up from his sleep, recalling two things that made him determined to leave and despite the pain, he began to walk. Divya stops him and assures him that once he's fully healed, they will complete the work together as he desired. Upon hearing this, he halts and demands to be taken home.

55

Chapter Fifty Five

Divya now sits next to Aryan, who is resting, when she receives a text saying, "We have caught the person responsible for the incident."

While reading, she glanced at Aryan, who was resting and holding her hand, and replied, "Please take good care of him until I come back."

Aryan, feeling better, leaves Divya at his place and sneaks off to college. Upon arrival, he entered the CEO's cabin in search of the recording. Upon witnessing something he couldn't tolerate, he discovered the identity of the culprit and immediately texted to arrange a meeting. After doing this, he waits and eventually Jahnavi appears. Aryan, upon seeing her, quickly plays the recording that captures her movements before the explosion occurred at his location. As she watches the recording, she falls into a contemplative silence, accepting responsibility for what transpired.

Upon learning this, Aryan chose not to ask any more questions and was leaving. In a low tone, she repeated the same line she had said to him earlier: "When anger takes over, even the clearest things appear blurry, even when they're right in front of your eyes."

Hearing the same word again, he faces her and says, "All this chaos just to ruin the cherished moment we had together, and now you can't handle it and have gone too far to erase that feeling."

He hands over the chip, the sole remaining copy, which contains their memories of being at his house. He mentioned that this is the final copy of the memories intended as a gift, but you corrected me, reminding me of your desire for hatred and an unchangeable heart. If this is your desire, let it be your eternal gift, a life of solitude where no one will attempt to mend your broken heart, as I have failed to do.

Jahnavi accepted everything as Divya asked, even though she hadn't done anything. Divya couldn't bear to watch their conversation any longer on the live recording, so she put the tablet aside and went to rest. After some time, Aryan comes back, his mind unable to find solace as he continues to reject all the proof he encountered today. Being tense, he noticed there was no way around leaving Divya. As she slowly regained her senses and couldn't feel his presence anymore, he approached her, holding her tightly, seeking solace. Divya, realizing that he was searching for comfort, held him even tighter, showing her care.

Divya finally got to hold him, but she remembers the terrible things she did in the past to make it happen. Aryan was targeted by someone who wanted revenge because Aryan insulted him for Jahnavi's sake and made his girlfriend his sister publicly. Moreover, this person intentionally took away Aryan's stardom and was planning something terrible for him. She trapped him in secret and won't let him go until she figures out how to separate Jahnavi and Akanchha from Aryan's life.

Earlier, when Jahnavi left her phone,

Jahnavi and Akanchha both left their belongings behind on the same day, and Divya took both items before heading towards the locked room where the main stud was trapped. When she arrived, she presented him with a tempting offer - an opportunity to seek revenge on Aryan but with one condition: i,e., without causing Aryan any harm, and she would assist him in achieving his desires.

He agreed to her terms while listening to her words, and then she gave him Aryan's lyrics and Jahnavi's phone to make it go viral. He sent a mail to the recommended studio partner from Jahnavi's phone. Then, she hands him Akanchha's details, already converted into a poster, instructing him to paste it everywhere, on which his sister's name is mentioned. Aryan and Jahnavi went their separate ways, while Akanchha had to resign for something she didn't do.

However, even after that, her work remained unfinished as she still didn't obtain what she desired. Therefore, she requested the main stud to secretly destroy all of Aryan's work. Divya had one last opportunity to destroy everything when Jahnavi walked into his spot to retrieve her belongings, and she asked Stud to burn the spot. However, Aryan couldn't find any evidence, as she had deleted the rest of the recording.

Finally, she reaches the point where Aryan was severely injured in the fire. Witnessing this, she commands her men to capture that bastard no matter what.

Present time,

Divya, when looked at the main stud who was chained up, she remembers Aryan worst health. She requested her men to treat him in the same way as Aryan felt.

"Please," he pleaded, "you can't do this. I've done everything you asked."

She responded, "I specifically requested that he not be harmed in any way, especially since he appears suspicious in the pre-planned explosion. I can't risk losing him, so it's only fair that you experience the same pain you caused Aryan. This way, he won't suspect you, which indirectly avoids any conflict for me."

She had her men tie him up with rope and throw him into the burning room. After a while, Divya instructed her men to retrieve him. They quickly pulled him out of the burning room, where his condition was even worse than Aryan's. By doing this, she felt calm and got her revenge for hurting Aryan. Plus, she eliminated the only suspect that could make Aryan suspicious of her. Then, she called Jahnavi and asked her to take all the blame, leaving Aryan with no escape but to turn to her. Divya, after all the efforts she made to get him back, finally got what she wanted and calmly fell asleep in his arms.

56

Chapter Fifty Six

Late in the morning,

While Aryan was still asleep, Divya attempted to wake him up. As she was about to leave the bed, he pulled her closer and asked her not to go. Even though Aryan was resting, Divya prepared beverages and waited for him in the evening, but he didn't come. Divya wanted to confront him about his odd behavior, but she discovered hidden files before she could approach him. She appeared annoyed when she realized he still had a copy of the shoot that she had already burned.

Fuming with anger, she stormed into his room and exclaimed, "Are you still working on the project I already cancelled? I managed to keep you safe and alive, but the thought of what could have happened in that fire scares me. Explain to me how you could be so negligent.

Aryan sat down and responded, "It's Akanchha's resignation."

She appears quiet, and he went on to say, "I'm aware you terminated her from the task."

She appeared shocked by how he found out and was a bit afraid of his reaction. With gentle care, he held her hand and said, "I don't need to know why, but let's start fresh and leave all the resentment behind."

Hearing the same word Anjali once used, she feels unvalued as he disregards her emotions, causing her to angrily withdraw her hand, stating, "It's not a mistake, and I won't change my decision. Everything will remain exactly as I want it, and you are restricted from working on any projects that are not ours. She openly admitted to being selfish this time, saying she doesn't want him involved in any work that makes her feel separated from him, and left.

During a meeting, Divya noticed a gathering at the main ground where Aryan had once again organized a beautifully decorated theme. Observing this, she appeared irritated and commanded her men to demolish everything. Aryan, who never opposes her orders, allowed it to happen again, silently leaving once it all fell apart, just like before.

He continuously develops new themes in various locations, only for her to eventually order their destruction. However, one day he decided to leave all the other places and chose his special spot at the back of the college. He added a few decorations around his favorite bench, transforming it into the perfect setting for an evening. Once everything was finished, he sat peacefully, observing the beauty of nature and waiting for someone. As evening approached, the special person failed to appear. Instead, he encountered Divya's staff and security, who were eagerly waiting for him to leave in order to dismantle the decorations. Aryan became annoyed when he saw everyone visiting his special place, so he decided to fight back for his cherished spot. Eventually, they clashed when they refused to yield to Aryan's opposition.

Upon arriving at college the following day, a sense of fear filled the air as everyone looked at the scene, until Divya came to investigate. When she arrived, she discovered that all her men and staff had been ruthlessly defeated. Upon seeing this, she received a text stating, "I attempted to give you a cherished memory that was only ours, but you don't deserve what you desired. In the end, I hope you to be happy."

When she read the last word "be happy," she glanced at the decoration that he had managed to save. Some of the staff, upon seeing the decoration, slowly regained their senses and attempted to destroy it, despite being injured. Divya ruthlessly struck them, demanding everyone to stay away from the area, while Jahnavi stopped her. Jahnavi instructed Divya's staff to clear the crowd. First, they cleared the spot, then Jahnavi escorted Divya away from there, leading her to the CEO cabin where she locked themselves inside.

Divya, still annoyed, angrily asked, "You're the one who tells him everything and makes things worse for me again."

Jahnavi shouted at her after hearing cruel words, "I followed all your instructions but everything ended in ruin because of your selfishness. Since you're not in a right state of mind, stay here until things improve outside."

Divya remained seated and Jahnavi left her for a moment. When she walked into the room, she noticed that Divya had exited through the back door. Jahnavi started searching for her, eventually finding her behind the wall, observing the mess she had unknowingly created. Now, everyone talks about the merciless attack she stubbornly pursued over a minor issue. Divya finally experienced the feeling of being ostracized, something Aryan felt daily.

Jahnavi grabs her hand and reassures her, "Don't pay attention to any of the nonsense they say. We can still handle everything to our advantage."

Divya said, "It's alright, someone once bestowed upon him the same feeling and torture as a gift, and now destiny repays that favor to me, which I embrace wholeheartedly. So, no need to think much about me. I will be fine."

As she wanted to be by herself, Jahnavi lets her walk to her cabin alone. Divya entered the room and played the recording, observing the unfortunate accident from last night. When she saw the recording, she appeared confused, wondering how everything had happened so suddenly. I had planned everything perfectly, so why did my plan backfire?

She pondered the same question repeatedly until late at night, when she finally left her cabin and headed to Aryan's special spot. When she arrived, she witnessed the destruction she had caused.

She kneels down and begins collecting all the broken items, especially the small gifts that Aryan wanted to give her. She tries her hardest to make things better, but in the end, everything seems worthless as they lack any emotion or sentiment like before.

In her fear of losing Aryan, Divya couldn't bring herself to leave the place and stayed there the entire night. When everyone returned to college, they found Divya sitting in the same spot, guarded by her staff and security. All eyes shifted towards her as she deliberately tried to sabotage everything Aryan did to elevate the college's standing.

57
Chapter Fifty Seven

For nearly 3 days, Divya has been coming to college, sitting in the same place, and not noticing anything. She appears completely disconnected from the outside world, lost in her own realm of sorrow. One day Aryan appeared out of nowhere while she was sitting alone, but she felt nothing when she saw him. Aryan notices her lost in thought and sits beside her in silence, both captivated by the beauty of nature. They remain in the same spot, sitting for a long time. Eventually, Divya drifts off to sleep.

On next day,

As soon as Divya woke up, she immediately noticed that Aryan had already left. She was about to leave too, but then she stopped and admired the even more beautiful decoration that had been set up again. She glanced around and spotted Aryan tying the last knot of the setup. She watched him, staying silent, then slowly passed him the broken items she had been holding since he left.

As he gazes at his broken gift, its meaning and precious feelings lost, the new present fails to evoke the same emotions. Consequently, all the preparation becomes meaningless to her, and without uttering a word, she departs, unwilling to create new memories. He noticed her ignoring everything because of his one mistake: ignoring her orders. He thought about how she had kept his broken gift safe and then left the spot. Upon returning, Divya notices that the decorations have been moved, clearing the spot.

After a while, she calmly settled back down in the same spot, and then Jahnavi and Akanchha joined her.

Not interrupting her, they both observed her silence as she absorbed the beauty of nature. Before leaving, Akanchha expressed her desire to see her return to her former self.

As she was leaving later at night, she suddenly halted to observe something strange. She commanded her men to leave her be, then hopped into a car driven by a special someone, without any objections. She arrives at the place she always loved and enters the house. Slowly, she walks up the stairs to the upper room, with her driver,that was Aryan, following behind. Finally, they reach his room where she climbs onto his bed while he sits a little distance away, watching her sleep all night.

She walks to her car upon waking up, waiting as she sees him approach to take her back to the same spot which she had gifted him. When Aryan observed her silent behavior, he felt powerless as she refused to express what was troubling her.

Aryan, finding himself without options, leaves her behind and proceeds towards the library, but hesitates when recalling his dismissal from all work, including accessing the library. While outside, he began searching for his belongings. Suddenly, he spotted his book upfront, which hadn't been there before. The hidden person, who didn't want to be confronted, had placed the item he was searching for. Just as he was about to grab it, he abruptly halts and turns around to find his sister waiting to talk.

Aryan left with his sister, leaving his belongings behind. He went to a locked site and secretly entered a room. After some time, he emerged with a few packages, which he handed to his sister. Aryan returned to the library side and discovered his belongings were gone. He stopped a girl coming out of the library and asked if she was the one present when he left his stuff.

She answered, "Your belongings are not my responsibility, and I have no interest in your matters." Just as she was leaving, she heard a voice from behind calling out, "Miss Trouble, it seems like there's still a lot more you're keeping hidden from me."

Listening this, she stops. He said, "I've noticed everything getting worse since I tried to change myself, but it seems like no one wants me to change even a little bit. Finally, I don't want false hope from someone who has already betrayed us when we needed her the most."

Jahnavi couldn't help but respond, "Your identity only brings hatred and miseries to everyone, whether you intentionally harm others. The negative consequences will always find you, and you can't deny it. This time, you treated your well-wisher worse. Whatever her condition is, it is all because of you.

He angrily grabs hold of her, while she looks afraid and meets his menacing gaze. She then slowly tells him, "You know it's entirely your fault, and there's nothing worse you can do to her now."

Aryan gradually distances himself from her as he refuses to accept the harsh truth. After exposing the truth, Jahnavi was about to depart, but before she left, she uttered, "You are the one who harmed her, and you are the only one who can restore her to her former self. I have faith in you." With those words, she departed.

Aryan, who had been left alone, spotted Divya standing in front and giving him the car keys to drive her home. Silently, he took the keys and brought her home. Upon entering the room, she settles on the bed while Aryan takes a seat. However, this time she gestures for him to come nearer instead of remaining silent or resting.

He climbs onto the bed, holding her close as they both drift off to sleep. He held her tighter, placing a kiss on her forehead as a blessing for everything she has done for him. Under her care, he drifted off to sleep. Aryan woke up late in the morning and realized Divya had already left. Rushing out of the house, he noticed that Divya's car was still parked by the door. He turned back to the house, searching everywhere for her, until finally, he approached the locked room.

Upon arrival, he noticed Divya standing by herself, marveling at the beautifully adorned decorations, exploring every corner of the room before eventually making his way toward the covered piano. Despite her efforts, she couldn't manage to uncover it. Aryan, unable to bear the sight of her abandoning everything she loved, retreated to his room. While lying down, all he can think about is whether she will come back or leave.

While contemplating, he suddenly recalls the night when he felt the same way about Jahnavi, who decided to leave. He closes his eyes tightly, overwhelmed by the fear of loneliness, but then feels a gentle touch on his heart, allowing her to come closer as he holds her tightly. Despite his fear of loneliness, he continues to close his eyes, prompting Divya to stay by his side and care for him.

58

Chapter Fifty Eight

It has been a few days since they both appeared, and in the meantime, Akanchha was given a few things by Aryan to keep them safe. After guarding the stuff for a long time, she couldn't resist and finally took a peek at it. Immediately, she covered it up as if nothing happened and was left pondering what to do next.

Jahnavi was concerned about something and tried calling Divya, but Akanchha abruptly ended the call, stating they needed to have a serious discussion.

Jahnavi appears shocked when she sees the stuff, as it's completely new to her. Akanchha shared, "My brother gave me his valuable things to keep safe, but I want to borrow some of them to repay his kindness. I should have done it earlier, and I need your assistance."

Jahnavi replied, "Before taking this step, consider the far-reaching consequences it will have on us and our college. If you've already made up your mind, I'll assist you. However, I must emphasize that if anything goes wrong this time, you'll be solely responsible."

Akanchha agreed to the terms without giving it a second thought. While Jahnavi took the stuff from her hand, she cautioned her about the potential consequences of their actions, warning that it could even ruin their sibling relationship.

Jahnavi sat alone in her villa, gazing at Aryan's belongings and the emotions he reserves for someone special. As soon as she read the precious name, "Anjali Pandey," her nerves exploded with the memories of their past interaction. Fueled by her intense hatred for Anjali, she angrily threw things around before isolating herself in her room.

Aryan and Divya have finally returned to the college. Divya appears calm as she resumes work, yet she tries to remain reserved. Aryan appears unsure about returning to college this time. Previously, he could effortlessly go to all the places he had visited, but now he tries to avoid the spots, feeling powerless. Whenever Divya takes him to his cherished places, he avoids looking around and only focuses on her hopeful and vibrant eyes, which he had almost lost in her.

Jahnavi finally arrived when she saw them returning. Divya appears calm now, unfazed by any potential disturbances. When Jahnavi discovers her former attitude, she appears happy for her and leaves the details on her desk, calling it a "welcome gift" that only she can handle correctly.

Divya casually disregarded it and left her cabin, searching for Aryan. She spotted him standing away from the library and froze, observing his movements and anticipating his next action. Aryan stood still, surveying all his cherished spots, then abruptly turned his back on everything and departed in silence.

During class, Aryan hears a sound he recognizes and abruptly leaves to track down the source of the tune. As he gets closer to the melody, his feelings turn for the worse and he hurries into the room. When he arrived, he noticed all three girls together. Akanchha was holding the camera, Jahnavi was practicing her steps, and Divya had returned to the piano and was playing his notes effortlessly.

In an instant, all his negative emotions vanished upon witnessing this. Divya raised her hand, prompting him to join her and play the notes he had neglected for so long. While he played, he appeared captivated by the melody, causing her to pause and step back a bit. While gazing into her eyes, he notices her eager desire to hear his words from the notes she prepared, understanding her wish, he begins to sing the song with affection.

Everyone's attention is drawn to Aryan singing for Divya, while the other girls in the room back off. As he gazes at her, completely captivated, he approaches and lovingly holds her by the waist. He incorporated her every little wish into his composition, revealing it all to her. He incorporated her every little wish into his composition, revealing it all to her. She appeared completely absorbed in him while listening, but suddenly interrupted him to prevent any further disclosure.

Aryan slowly regained his senses and noticed everyone around him seemed captivated by his song. He then shifted his gaze to Divya, who initially appeared fine but now seemed tense and angry. Without uttering another word, she abruptly left the area. As she departed, he noticed Jahnavi gathering her belongings, and finally glanced at his sister who appeared anxious about his transformation. Before he could address her, Jahnavi quickly took hold of her hand and they left together.

Aryan, surrounded by the crowd, appears tense, contemplating the sudden departure of the girls, each with a different reaction to his song. When everyone else had gone, Aryan was still there, and then Akanchha showed up just before it was too late. By gazing into her eyes, he could decipher her emotions and the questions that all revolved around Anjali. Aryan remains quiet, but eventually she speaks up, saying, "I hope you haven't forgotten about her."

As he hears this, he suddenly recalls the night and his words, "I need you more, my 'well-wisher'." As he remembers this, he shuts his eyes to avoid confronting her afterwards. Shortly after Akanchha departed, he noticed Divya leaving the college as well, without him. As he was departing, his thoughts shifted to the items he had given to Akanchha. But then, a sudden realization struck him - the lines and tune that Divya had played were actually a modified rendition of his own composition. He was left wondering who else has access to his belongings.

When Divya arrived at her villa, she meticulously examined every corner before finally seeking solace in her sister's room. While being there, she felt a strong desire to express her current emotions. When she no longer felt her sister's presence, she became tense, realizing that she needed her the most but she wasn't there. Even though she hesitated, she eventually settled down on her sister's chair and spent the entire night lost in thought about her.

59
Chapter Fifty Nine

When Aryan arrived at college, he noticed Divya sitting in the same spot again. He walked towards her and found her looking at some sketches. Gazing at him, she softly inquired, "Do you not love me more than I could ever love myself?"

She showed him the sketch in which he had captured the moment of her sitting at the same spot, waiting for him. While revealing the sketch, her gaze only met his eyes, which witnessed nothing but her care. Leading him by the hand, she guides him to the library side. Despite being present, he refuses to look at his prized spot, but she eventually hands him the modified contract. The former contract, authorized by his late aunt, allowed him to work in the library. Now, the new CEO, Divya, has given her consent and officially appointed him as the librarian again.

Aryan examined the altered contract as she uttered, "Now, nothing can prevent you from accessing any part of this college and experiencing any emotion that is safeguarded here."

He glanced at everyone whose perception of Divya was gradually shifting. He gradually accepted the contract while observing. Once he agrees to the terms, everyone commends Divya for her efforts to change her past actions. Divya, who received blessings from all, promised a big celebration before their first semester.

Aryan, who finally could move into his cherished place, was about to enter the library after a long time when he suddenly paused, thinking about his lost diary. As if he entered the library, there's a chance she'll ask for the return of her feelings that she left with him. He changed his mind, retraced his steps, and then walked in a certain direction, with her mimicking his movements. Once they arrived at the spot, Aryan stopped and took a moment to appreciate the bike he had been given. Then he turned to her and extended his hand, indicating that he wanted his gift back. As she watched, she took out the keys and handed them to him, her eyes filling with tears. He openly asked for his gift back, which he had already left when he left her.

He looked into her tear-filled eyes and gently whispered, "From now on, only beautiful memories await us." Listening to this, she seems calm.

While he rides away on his bike, Divya, who still has much to do, heads towards the meeting room. When she arrived, she noticed that everyone she had called in advance was already there. Divya settled on her chair and Akanchha proposed her new project, unveiling the photos she had taken the previous day. Aryan and Divya's portfolio, which she accidentally captured and transformed into a portrait for their new campaign. Divya, appearing lost, declared, "I designate you as the lead for our upcoming task. You have full access to any resources you need for your assignment from our company to ensure it's completed before the 1st semester. There should be no delays after this."

She commanded everyone to return to their work. Divya urged Jahnavi to stay after seeing Akanchha leaving. Divya, who was alone, took out a few other samples besides Akanchha's collection. She had been safeguarding the missing portrait of Aryan and Jahnavi, eagerly awaiting this moment. Divya silently conveyed her message to Jahnavi by finally returning her lost memories, indicating that she is unwilling to share him with anyone, even in her dreams.

Jahnavi silently takes the portrait with her after understanding the clear message. Just before heading to her villa, she halted and gazed at the portrait, her eyes welling up with tears, as it held countless cherished memories with Aryan. She finally threw it in the dustbin and left, never to see it again. Divya, observing from a distance, finally defeated the last person who dared to dream of a life with Aryan.

Witnessing her shattered desires, she finally departs in agony. Feeling a sense of tranquility, she sets everything aside and proceeds towards the cursed house. Upon arrival, she locked the main gate and proceeded directly to her room. Upon entering the room, she locked it and turned around to find Aryan waiting for her. Afterward, she stands there, observing the desired look on his face, before slowly undressing herself step by step as she approaches him. Finally, all she had left was undergarments, which made Aryan's desire apparent, but she still waited for him to reveal his true intentions.

He sits down, signaling her to treat him well, and she complies by getting on top of him. Aryan desired to feel the essence of love caressing her body, starting from her naked skin and passing through her heart. As he moves downward, he slips his hand inside her underwear and playfully teases her with one hand while holding her neck, making her gaze into his eyes. He wants to test how much she desires it, and when she reaches her limit, she climaxes and embraces him tightly. Observing her, he reduces his speed and meets her gaze directly, as she utters, "I want you to take care of me however you desire." With those words, she kisses him and intensifies her efforts to fulfill his every whim.

Aryan responds to her by passionately kissing and biting her, creating intense sensations as their bodies and desires collide. Divya slowly undressed him, and once he was completely naked, Aryan removed the last piece of clothing from her. Aryan and Divya engage in a passionate lovemaking session after undressing each other. As she becomes wilder, he treats her even more rudely, fulfilling his desires until she nearly reaches climax and abruptly stops. Upon seeing this, Aryan openly expressed his need for her, repeating the same word, "I need you more, my 'well-wisher'."

Hearing this, her excitement grew even more than she get on top of him. Aryan's excitement grew as he looked into her eyes, wanting to have her his way. She could sense his desires and pleased him with her care. Aryan spent the entire night with her on one bed, completely sober, which had never happened before. Left alone, his thoughts filled with the fear that Divya, too, would abandon him like everyone else. First Anjali, then Jahnavi, and now it's Divya. With these thoughts, he closes his eyes, feeling a shiver of fear at the prospect of being left behind once more.

Just as he's about to lose all hope, Divya comes back to him, slowly embracing him and holding him tighter. Aryan finds a glimmer of hope when Divya's warmth and care make him feel alive again.

Opening his eyes gradually, he saw Divya in front of him. Despite her own pain, she forgot about it the moment she saw him helpless. Upon seeing this, Aryan tightly hugged her. Finally, she spoke to him and revealed her wish, saying, "I need you."

When Aryan hears this word, he finishes by saying, "my 'well-wisher'."

Aryan finally remembers the girl he thinks about every night, Divya, who takes care of him during his worst moments, and can no longer bear to see her in pain. Then, he repeats the same words, his voice filled with desperation, "I need you, my 'well-wisher'."

Absorbing every sound, Divya's grip on him tightened, coaxing him to settle on her. Meeting his gaze, she spoke softly, "To feel alive again, I need your tender care."

Aryan kissed her on the lips and they indulged in passionate lovemaking, satisfying all their desires. As she slowly returned to her former state, she was overcome with pleasure, climaxing not once, but twice. Witnessing Aryan engaging in intimate acts while being fully aware, she was taken aback. "I require your presence even more," Aryan said.

As she listened to his wish, she straddled him, fully surrendering herself to him in the act of love-making. When Aryan reminisced about everything, he glanced to her side, where she peacefully rested. He sat there, observing her, lost in thought about his past self and the transformation he underwent to revive her. One thought consumes his mind: "What will I say to her when she reenters my life?"

60

Chapter Sixty

It has been a few days since they both came back to college, where everyone was getting ready for the big event. Divya intended to keep Aryan away from college and stay with him at his house until the day before the upcoming grand event. Without warning, Akanchha summoned Aryan for a serious discussion. Divya tightly holds his hand as she watches him leave, her eyes filled with longing. While he was leaving, memories of the day he left flooded his mind. That day, when he returned to the house, he was startled to find Anjali gone.

The memory makes him reluctant to leave. Divya attempted to persuade him, but he adamantly refused to leave her side. However, when she opened the door, he was met with armed forces protecting the house. He appears calm as he looks at all this, but suddenly he turns and says, "No matter what happens, you won't leave this place. I can't bear the thought of losing you, not even in my dreams."

Seeing him still fearful brings back memories of the night he lost Anjali. While calmly holding his hand, she assures him, "I'll be right here when you come back. I won't leave this house until then, so please don't keep me waiting too long."

Finally convinced by her words, he heads off to meet his sister. Meanwhile, Jahnavi sneaks into the previously locked site where all the details of the former campaign are stored. She continues her search for a specific detail that she believes is only here.

Eventually, she discovers the details on the desk and quickly grabs the file, but abruptly pauses to survey the chaotic surroundings. Everything is in disarray, except for the desk and the file, which remain untouched. As she reflects on the situation, she quickly realizes she is not alone. Out of nowhere, she quickly pulled out the gun and aimed it at the person standing behind her. Despite being held at gunpoint, he refuses to stop, leading her to angrily aim the gun at his heart, which only makes him more aggressive.

As he descended into madness, he no longer cared about himself, causing her to reluctantly lower her gun and was leaving. He surprised her by grabbing her hand from behind and said, "Miss Trouble, it seems like you're still keeping a lot from me."

Gripping his collar tightly, she angrily questions, "Are you joking with me? I ran to find you because I thought you might be in pain or something worse had happened to you.

"Because you've cared for me since we first met," he continued.

As she listened, she remained silent. Moving closer, he added, "I just realized that it was you who orchestrated everything - from convincing me to go back to college, to sacrificing the song I wrote for you to help my sister with her assignment. You turned my tune for someone else into a favor for Divya, even fighting with her to restore my sister's prestige at the project. When you gave Divya the lead role for the new campaign, you almost sacrificed your memories, which used to be your place. Finally, you decided to find me after receiving my message about being hurt. Don't you feel any pain or concern, even when I'm right beside you?

With tears in her eyes, she responded, "I only feel hatred towards you. When you're near, I feel completely powerless. I need you to disappear from my life and never appear, even when I'm in distress or require your support. Consider this my sole desire, beyond which I require nothing from you."

Granting her wish, he kissed her forehead and handed her the final gift. He expressed his desire for a friend like her, someone who would always support him as she did for his sister and his well-wisher. Despite this, he was happy for her that she would no longer have to tolerate his presence. Despite the many bad memories I've given you, the time we spent together in my cursed house was the most precious and will always be cherished in my heart. Finally, my wish for you is eternal happiness.

Jahnavi takes a look at the last gift he left, which happens to be the same portrait she discarded. Unable to bear the pain, she cried out, consumed by thoughts of his actions towards her. Divya, who had been waiting for Aryan, sat and stared at the door all night, but he never came back. Glancing at the clock, she noticed there was only a short amount of time left for the grand celebration. Upon seeing this, she quickly left a note for Aryan and headed off to college.

Upon arrival, she noticed everyone was there but couldn't locate the two girls. She tries to call Akanchha, but her number appears to be unreachable. Then, she attempts to call Jahnavi, who also doesn't answer any calls. Noticing everyone's absence, she appeared concerned as she remained unaware of the impending chaos at the concert.

The crowd eagerly anticipating the new composition release watched as the studio manager and his staff entered the location. Everyone appears shocked, wondering what brought them to this concert. Divya observes them approaching with their troop, but remains silent as the studio brings its own equipment, including luxury vehicles for transporting the heavy musical gear and speakers. As soon as they reached the stage, they immediately began setting up their equipment. Divya appeared annoyed upon seeing this, and just as she was about to intervene, the last car pulled in and Aryan emerged.

Aryan, noticing everyone's amazement, quietly approached his well-wisher, who seemed annoyed at first but appeared calm when he approached. Aryan walked towards the stage with Divya, holding her hand, and sat on the piano seat. There, she saw new musical notes, which were his new composition tune. Eagerly anticipating, she began the concert with a warm welcome, swiftly transitioning to playing the first notes of Aryan's composition, prompting him to sing without hesitation. Once she finished the first composition, she seamlessly transitioned to the second playlist, maintaining the flow. Aryan then fervently continued singing his second composition.

After completing the second composition, everyone praised him. The studio partner was pleased with the release of three compositions under their name, as they had initially only expected one. Both the studio and the audience were amazed. After finishing playing the notes, Divya quietly left, but he grabbed her hand while singing the final song that is meant just for her. She interrupted him from expressing his feelings about her when she heard the lyrics, but this time, she couldn't stop him.

Singing, Aryan locks eyes with her, baring his heart and reminiscing about their shared experiences. While he was singing the song, the company portal finally launched the new campaign poster. The poster was completely based on the live song that Aryan is currently singing, and all the rights belong to Divya Shukla. Upon seeing the poster, everyone showered blessings upon the couple as the lyrics, creating a profound impact on all.

His studio partner, who wanted the cover page for himself, approached Aryan, and asked if he would like to be the lead model for his latest 3 albums. As there's no one else who could replace him in his eyes.

Without Aryan's consent, Divya took his hand and convinced him to sign the contract. The studio finally did something good for Aryan, and the concert crowd praised them.

Divya kissed Aryan's cheeks and said, "I am blessed to be your well-wisher, as you turned all my wishes into reality in just one day. I don't want this day to end, and I wish time would freeze right now."

Hearing this, he kissed her forehead and said, "I wish I could freeze this moment for you, but I don't want to remember it as it is the end of our story."

61

Chapter Sixty One

With a shocking look, she turned to his side as he finished his last word, and in an instant, his caring nature transformed into anger. He swiftly pulled her onto his back, simultaneously stopping the deadly mob attempting to attack Divya from behind. Divya spotted Aryan and noticed a growing armed mob approaching him. Meanwhile, her security force intervenes to bring down the mob.

In an instant, the once pleasant concert ground transforms into a battlefield. As the crowd fled to save themselves, Divya, who was searching for a safe way out, suddenly stopped when she saw the leader of the mob approaching, the same person she had already taken care of.

Witnessing his return, she immediately called for armed forces to intervene, as the stud was not alone this time and had a massive force backing him up. In an instant, he gained complete control of the college. Aryan, who was managing the situation, abruptly halts as he notices his sister held at gunpoint near the projector. The main stud, who covers half of his face, walks calmly to his side, catching his attention. Once again, standing in front, he removed the mask from his face, unveiling his half-burned face, and asked, "Do you know what this is?"

While Aryan stayed quiet, he went on to say, "This is a gift from your well-wisher who told me to kill you."

Aryan froze in place as the stud continued speaking. "Not only did she cleverly involve your sister in this war game, but she also attempted to harm your previous campaign's lead model and even tried to kill me. I follow her every command, giving her everything she desires, but no longer, as I am here to seek revenge on everyone who wronged me and my boss."

Aryan glanced behind him and saw the ex-manager, now free from his trap. Everyone appeared terrified when they saw him, except for Aryan who burst into laughter. However, his laughter quickly turned into anger as he clenched the stud's neck and said, "I've known everything from the beginning, including what's been happening behind my back and even today." I let you free to show up in here so that we can finally take you down once and for all."

In a single shot, Aryan takes down the person, breaking his neck, as the ex-manager silently observes and then looks around in shock, repeating, "Finally, we can take them down." He quickly realizes it's a trap and commands his men to shoot at him. He begins running aimlessly, drawing the entire crowd to chase after him, causing the remaining people to flee in order to save themselves.

The entire ground cleared out, leaving only the mob, Divya, her security force, and Aryan. At that moment, the mob leader halts all gunfire. When he realized he was trapped in the mental game, he burst out laughing and said, "You're really clever when faced with adversity. If you don't come yourself, I'll bring this place down and go to your sister instead."

Aryan, who has already left, still hasn't appeared despite the final warning. The head of the mob seemed aggravated and instructed his crew to open fire in order to demolish this place.

Without delay, they unleashed heavy gunfire on the college's architecture and its most precious locations. They had been doing this for a while, but even though everything got messed up, Aryan still didn't show up. Eventually, he decided to forcefully bring his sister to the ground. They bring his sister to the main area, where she is now being held at gunpoint. Just as he was about to shoot, Divya stepped in and warned, "I stayed quiet when you damaged my belongings, but if you take another step, I guarantee none of you will make it out alive."

Laughing, he said, "Miss CEO, just so you know, every route to this college is blocked and your little security force won't be able to defeat my army. I came here solely to seek revenge from him, so step back."

Even so, she remains unwilling to step away and fearlessly takes hold of Akanchha's hand, ready to leave. The mob leader aimed his gun at her, then shifted his aim towards Aryan, who was boiling with anger at the sight of him and the threat he posed to his loved ones. The mob leader, driven by his hatred, set his gun aside and declared, "We must resolve a few matters since you've taken care of me. Now it's my turn to repay you. Recall that you once challenged a politician to land 10 blows on you, and if you stayed stationary, it would settle everything. In this round, we'll play the same game, but with my rules. Your chances of succeeding will be doubled.

Upon hearing this, his crew initiates an attack on Aryan, one by one. Initially, he tries to defend himself, but as he realizes that over 10 people are targeting him simultaneously, multiplying their movements by over 10 times, he understands that ethics have no place here. Aryan then tries to retreat, but he can't endure it any longer. Slowly and mercilessly, he was brought down, finally falling to his knees. It was then that the leader of the mob emerged for a one-on-one battle. Despite being broken, Aryan remained motionless as he swiftly drew his gun, declaring, "Let's finish this game right here."

Uttering this, he pulled the trigger. Everyone seemed terrified as Akanchha screamed upon seeing her brother get shot. Aryan, who believed he was being shot, cautiously places his hand on his chest and feels his heartbeat, confirming he was alive. While the sound of the gunshot took aback the mob leader, he hadn't even pulled the trigger yet. So, who else could it be?

Then everyone's attention shifted to the other side where Divya was holding an antique gun and fired shots. This annoyed the leader of the mob, who said, "I already warned you, princess, you won't win this game today." With a smile, he placed the gun against his heart, surrounded by his men who had almost taken over her security, and said, "Let this be our last encounter, for it has been an honor to face a worthy opponent like you."

Aryan glanced at his well-wisher and sister, smiling reassuringly to convey that everything will be fine. Just as he was about to pull the trigger, a blade completely severed his right hand, the one holding the gun aimed at Aryan. He screamed in agony as he saw his hand being cut off. Not finding anyone responsible, his crew redirects the heavy war machine towards the person on the left and prepares to attack, but abruptly halts upon hearing the increasingly loud parade march. Upon hearing this, the entire crew became alert and positioned themselves in all directions as a massive parade emerged from every corner and made its way to the main ground.

The crew responds to their heavy weaponry by opening fire, and in turn, they retaliate with a few bombs and toxic gas. The army took down almost the entire crew with just 1-2 shots, watching his men die. Then, with his other hand, he activated the bomb planted in a different part of the college. Each blast now blocks the paths they were using to reach the main ground.

62
Chapter Sixty Two

He remains motionless, observing the obstructed path, which remains silent for a moment, until a series of deafening blasts that reverberate through the entire area startles everyone, engulfing the ground in a cloud of dust. Eventually, when everything became clear, the mob leader found himself alone while his men lay defeated, surrounded by unfamiliar soldiers. Terrified of a horrifying demise, he opts to sacrifice himself rather than becoming their prey. He contemplated pointing the gun at himself, ready to pull the trigger, but couldn't go through with it. He glanced at the trigger, halted by someone in front of him. He saw Jahnavi, who angrily declared, "I was the one who freed you once, but now I'll set you free forever."

Pulling out the antique gun, she displayed the exact one that Divya owns, distinguished by the emblem seen on the massive parade suits and all their machinery. As he faced death head-on, he smiled and declared, "This game was worth winning because I took him down, just as I intended. Finally, I am proud to have an honorable death."

Upon hearing his last words, Jahnavi pulled the trigger and shot him. Jahnavi noticed everyone's terrified expressions and felt a strange sensation. She turned slowly, only to be shocked by the sight of Aryan angrily plunging a broken blade into his chest while holding Jahnavi's gun in his other hand, causing it to shoot wildly.

Filled with hatred and seeking revenge, Aryan angrily removed the blade and ultimately killed the leader of the mob.

Jahnavi slowly released her grip from the gun that Aryan now holds. The pain and burning desire for vengeance does not diminish Aryan hatred. In a sudden twist, the army general violently seizes the antique gun from Aryan, declaring, "This is for the leader alone. You are nothing more than an ordinary boy who can't even face one of my soldiers."

Aryan, in a fit of anger, retaliated with his broken blade and all his might, but was saved by his fellow crew. However, before they could recover, Aryan attacked them again with triple the force and moves, taking down three of their members. The force was so intense that even the leader stepped back, only to find the gun missing and now in Aryan's hand. He removed his shield in order to fight back. Aryan, despite being broken, remained strong and fought back. The leader and his army advanced towards Aryan to reclaim the gun.

Aryan aims the gun at the leader, but before he can shoot, he is unexpectedly stabbed in the back with the same blade. He felt pain and eventually knelt down. When he looked at the person, it turned out to be Jahnavi, who intentionally stabbed him in the back. She then stood before the army, raising her hand with the supreme emblem marked on it. The entire parade came to a halt and knelt before Jahnavi, who commanded, "Clear the area and eliminate any recordings or witnesses of this moment."

Every single person is being dug out by the soldiers, and each recording of the site was brought, while they wait for her final order. Jahnavi, who had almost lost her sanity after witnessing so many terrible things in just one day, was on the verge of ordering their execution. Aryan whispered to her from behind, "Don't let anyone hate you, as you've always wanted. Let this be a gift solely for me, not for anyone else."

She kneels down and holds his face, making eye contact, before swiftly pulling out the blade. In agony, he screamed just as the explosion erupted on her back, obliterating the only evidence of this horrific event. With her hands, she covers Aryan's wound while gripping him. Once everything was resolved, Jahnavi stated, "You can't give up so easily, as there's much more you have to endure."

She retrieved her gun from him and promptly handed it to the leader, who immediately shot the mob leader and then shot the stud that Aryan had already killed. Jahnavi managed to save him from the accusation of death by stating, "I have repaid all your kindness by ensuring that my people will handle everything that happened here."

The moment she finished her sentence, she realized she was being held at gunpoint by Divya. Who said, "You purposely released the beast that I was guarding the day Aryan put it in? You purposely orchestrated all of this to cause me pain, and this time, you've succeeded. However, it ends today."

As the army prepared to intervene, she loaded the gun. Jahnavi stopped and braced herself for what was to come, looking into Aryan's eyes with a smile that seemed to indicate she had longed for this moment. Just as Divya was about to shoot, she heard a voice say, "I'm the one who set him free."

"I noticed something suspicious inside the college while I was on my way to meet my sister," he continued. "I discovered that there will be a major conflict at the concert today in an attempt to remove their leader from this location. To prevent anything worse from happening, I decided to release the chief after witnessing how much the concert arrangement meant to you. I reached out to Jahnavi for assistance and she only completed the tasks I requested. I expected everything to go smoothly, but in the end, I realized they never returned for me. They only came for you because you were the one with the key to the main chamber I was guarding when I came back to college. When I couldn't save it anymore, I gave the key to my sister to take it away. I just found out that it was this stud who has been watching my every move from the beginning and released all the campaign details in Jahnavi's name. He planned to use you as bait to seek revenge on me, and finally, he kidnapped my sister in an attempt to obtain the key, which you always kept safe as my bike key ring."

He revealed the hidden key inside his bike key ring. Divya closes her eyes while losing the gun, discovering the truth behind this massive chaos. In pain, fear causes her to shiver as she thinks the disaster was her fault. Aryan, unsure of how to explain her pain, cautiously approached and said, "It's all over now. You won't be hurt as long as I'm around."

As he reached out to hold her hand, she slapped him hard and pushed him away, shouting through tears, "You've destroyed everything, and now everyone will see you as a criminal! I cannot permit you to continue your education at this college after this. You are prohibited from participating in the session except for taking your exam, after which you must leave."

Aryan was in disbelief when she explicitly told him to leave her and the college. Silently, Aryan retreats and walks towards the lifeless body of the stud. Once there, he retrieves his final belongings from his coat - his blood-soaked diary. Carrying it, he returned to Divya and said, "You never asked me anything, and when you finally did, you requested the worst gift for yourself." Finally, he handed her the diary and said, "Stay happy and safe, as I am departing."

With tear-filled eyes, he kissed her forehead immediately, even though she still refused to meet his gaze. As he spoke his final words, he raised his hand towards his sister, and together they departed.

As Divya slowly opened her eyes, she saw him leaving and he was almost at the college gate. She couldn't believe that she asked him to leave her, which she now regrets, and she starts running after him to stop him. Seeing this, Jahnavi order to block her path. Half of the army formed a solid wall, with Aryan departing from their back side and only Jahnavi and Divya standing in front. Witnessing them obstructing her path, Divya loses her sanity and begins shooting every person who stands in her way, knowing that touching her would result in a painful death due to the commander clan's antique gun she possesses.

They gradually cleared a path for her to walk, only for her to be injected with a tranquilizer just as she was about to call out Aryan's name. Jahnavi, who is stone-hearted, persists in injecting the serum despite the pain of being abandoned. Falling unconscious, she slowly collapsed into Jahnavi's arms as everything before her eyes turned blurry. Jahnavi whispered, "It's time for you to rest, little princess. I promise to fix everything for you exactly as you wished when you wake up."

Holding Jahnavi tightly, she then passed out. With tears in her eyes, Jahnavi looked around at the mess that Divya had been preparing for so long, only for it to all turn to ashes in one day. Seeing this, she couldn't help but curse Aryan, blaming him for everything, and yelling, "You are just as evil as Anjali, and I will make sure you lose everything. Divya only took your happiness, but I will go further and remove your soul from your body as punishment for your actions towards her today."

63

Chapter Sixty Three

The college premises were closed a few days ago after its license expired and it came under jurisdiction with several charges, but no one showed up to defend it. Several files were eventually delivered to the courtroom. Upon reviewing the details, everyone appeared shocked. When they finally closed the file, they saw the long-lost antique emblem from the city, causing everyone to withdraw the charges they had previously made. The lawyer representing the college asked the judge, who seemed scared by the logo, to grant clearance for the college to operate under favorable conditions on behalf of the client, "Elite group of companies."

The judge silently signed the clean chit for the college upon hearing the company name, without any objections. With a clean chit in hand, he left the court and drove directly to the secure mansion where Jahnavi awaited the outcome. Upon arriving, he presented her with the clean chit, and seeing it, she appeared calm as she finally had something to bring Divya to her senses and revive her.

Divya, who had completely lost her mind since that day, finds herself back in the same state from which Aryan had once rescued her, now sitting outside the college and staring at the ceiling above the main gate. It seems like she's worried that if college doesn't start again, there won't be semester exams, and as a result, Aryan won't return.

She always arrives during college hours and stays until the end, with her men and staff constantly watching her. Regardless of the weather, she remains there, pondering what would happen if Aryan came and she wasn't there to apologize for her mistake. Suddenly, Jahnavi's men appeared and immediately broke the sealing. Divya, upon seeing this, decides to intervene and Jahnavi hands her the court order. Even though she remained quiet, she eventually made her way into college. Divya and Jahnavi witnessed complete devastation as they arrived at the college grounds, with the entire architecture of the building ruthlessly destroyed.

Divya finally spoke, her voice filled with sorrow, "once a beautiful place now reduced to ashes."

She commanded her men to begin repairing the building. After a few days, everything was restored to its original state and the college reopened for exams. Divya, who eagerly anticipates this day, remains seated at her usual spot, waiting for Aryan, but he never appears. Despite waiting, Divya still hopes that he will come to collect his last paper, but Aryan doesn't show up for the final exam either.

Divya eventually acknowledged that he has moved on and will not come back to her, as she had desired. Despite setting up the place as he wanted, she couldn't find him and grew increasingly unsettled. She set fire to her favorite place, which she had previously gifted to Aryan. While doing so, she also approaches his bike to set it on fire. However, she notices Jahnavi standing in front of her and hears her say, "Don't recklessly destroy everything for just one thing. There are many more things to take care of, so be cautious."

Amidst the raging fire, Divya's voice trembled with anger as she confronted Jahnavi. "My heart is wounded," she said, "and it can only heal if he cares for me. I can't do it because I have no idea where he has been. I can't find any trace of him to bring him back into my life, but you wouldn't understand this feeling because you've never been as close to him as I have."

Just before she left, Jahnavi turned to ask, "What if I make it my mission to track him down?"

Divya disregards what she said and departs. Jahnavi hasn't been to college for 2 days, but one day when Divya was leaving for her villa, she saw Jahnavi waiting with some files. As she approaches, she hands over the file. As Divya looks at Aryan's recent picture, tears fill her eyes while she examines every detail of him. "Is it worth any price to have him back in your life?" Jahnavi questioned."

As Divya listened to her words, she felt a growing sense of assurance that she could bring him back, as long as she offered a compelling deal. Contemplating their mission, she spoke assertively, "We cannot delay, we have business to take care of."

After spending some time in the meeting room, Jahnavi and Divya emerged and found Jahnavi's car waiting outside, ready to take them to their destination. When Jahnavi leaves, she stops hearing Divya's voice, who said, "He's scared of dark and lonely nights, so please take good care of him if necessary. But I want him back in this college at any cost. Until then, I'll be waiting."

~The End~

9 798894 467580